A Wonderful Thing

"Could I listen to your heart for a second? I never listened to anyone's heart."

He nodded and she rested her head lightly against his chest, listening.

"It sounds so alive," she whispered. He didn't say anything, trembling.

"Are you okay?" she sat up. He nodded.

"What's wrong?"

"No one ever—" He took a deep breath. "You sounded like it was—special."

"That you're alive?" He nodded.

"Well it is." She rested her fingertips just below the hollow where his collarbones met.

"It's really special."

Other Avon Flare Books by
Ellen Emerson White

FRIENDS FOR LIFE

Avon Books are available at special quantity discounts for bulk purchases for sales promotions, premiums, fund raising or educational use. Special books, or book excerpts, can also be created to fit specific needs.

For details write or telephone the office of the Director of Special Markets, Avon Books, 959 8th Avenue, New York, New York 10019, 212-262-3361.

Romance is a Wonderful Thing

Ellen Emerson White

AN AVON FLARE BOOK

ROMANCE IS A WONDERFUL THING is an original publication of Avon Books. This work has never before appeared in book form.

Excerpt from LIGHT IN AUGUST by William Faulkner Copyright 1932 and renewed in 1960 by William Faulkner, Random House, Inc.

Excerpts from LONG DAY'S JOURNEY INTO NIGHT by Eugene O'Neill used by permission of Yale University.

Selections from "The Music Man" by Meredith Willson Copyright © 1957 FRANK MUSIC CORP. and RINIMER CORPORATION International Copyright Secured. All Rights Reserved. Used by Permission.

Excerpt from WHO'S AFRAID OF VIRGINIA WOOLF? by Edward Albee, reprinted by permission of William Morris Agency, Inc. on behalf of the author.

AVON BOOKS
A division of
The Hearst Corporation
959 Eighth Avenue
New York, New York 10019

Copyright © 1983 Ellen Emerson White
Published by arrangement with the author
Library of Congress Catalog Card Number: 83-4627
ISBN: 0-380-83907-5

All rights reserved, which includes the right to reproduce this book or portions thereof in any form whatsoever except as provided by the U. S. Copyright Law. For information address Walter Pitkin Agency, 11 Oakwood Drive, Weston, Connecticut 06883

Library of Congress Cataloging in Publication Data
White, Ellen Emerson.
  Romance is a wonderful thing.

  (An Avon/Flare book)
  Summary: An honor student and a high school "clown" are increasingly attracted to each other, though the ensuing gossip threatens their relationship.
  I. Title
PZ7.W58274Ro 1983   [Fic]   83-4627
ISBN 0-380-83907-5

First Flare Printing, July, 1983

FLARE BOOKS TRADEMARK REG. U. S. PAT. OFF. AND IN OTHER COUNTRIES, MARCA REGISTRADA, HECHO EN U. S. A.

Printed in the U. S. A.

WFH 10 9 8 7 6 5 4 3 2 1

*To Ebony,
who dances among sugarplums*

CHAPTER ONE

Patricia Masters, usually called Trish, hurried down the crowded high school corridor, well on her way to being late for trigonometry class. She was sixteen, thin, with summer-bleached blond hair and a perpetual eyebrows-lifted expression of good-humored confusion.

"Slow down, we've got plenty of time." Janet Casey, one of her best friends, pulled her back.

"I guess." Trish checked between the pages of her math book to make sure she had a pen. "Did you study for this?"

"A little." Janet shrugged. "It's not going to be hard."

"Yeah, sure." Trish flipped her hair over her shoulders. "I shouldn't even bother going."

"She said she was going to drop the lowest quiz."

"She's going to have a hard time choosing." Trish started up the stairs to the second floor of the old building.

"Oh, come on, you have like a B average—"

"Hey, don't forget, you guys." A boy passing them touched Janet's arm. "Yearbook meeting after school."

"We have a tennis match," Trish said.

"*We* have a deadline," the boy called over his shoulder.

"*We* have a problem." Trish glanced at her friend, who didn't even hear.

"He's so cute," Janet sighed.

"Is your arm on fire where he touched it?"

"Oh, funny." Janet touched the spot above her elbow absently. "We have to go to that meeting, Trish—we'll have time before the bus leaves."

"You mean, we'll *make* time."

Janet nodded.

As Trish followed her down the hall, a boy with unruly

dark hair and a tilted grin crashed into her, knocking her books out of her arms.

"Hey, sorry." His grin got more arrogant as he bent down to pick the books up. "Trig?" He handed it to her. "What are you, a brain?"

"N-no." Trish shook her head. "I'm sorry, I wasn't looking where I was—"

"Don't worry about it, kid." He ran his eyes up and down, and grinned again.

"Mac, come on!" one of his friends shouted from down the hall.

"Yeah, right." He gave her another one of her books. "Not a brain, huh? Later." He jogged after his friends.

"Kid?" Trish stared after him, irritated. "He's a junior too."

"He's a jerk, that's what he is," Janet said. "Colin McNamara is the last person whose opinion I'd worry about."

"Yeah, I guess," Trish said. "Hey, are we late?"

Janet peered at the clock inside the classroom they were passing.

"Yeah, we are," she said.

"Hey, I'm home!" Trish yelled, dropping her tennis racket and books on the chair in the front hall of her family's town house on Commonwealth Avenue, in the center of Boston's Back Bay section.

"Did you win?" Her mother's voice floated out from the kitchen.

"Wasn't it nice out today?" Trish bent down and patted their basset hound, who was asleep at the bottom of the stairs. "Hi, Freud."

The dog opened his eyes, thumped his tail twice, and went back to sleep.

"We got smashed," Trish said as she continued on to the kitchen. "They had a really good team."

Her mother, also blond, and with the same expressive

eyebrows, looked up from her book. "How did you do personally?"

"Actually, I won." Trish took an apple out of the fruit bowl. "I think the girl I played had the flu."

Mrs. Masters smiled. "What was the score?"

"Six-two, six-nothing." She leaned into the refrigerator. "My serves were going in pretty well. How come we never buy Tab?"

"How come you never drink orange juice?"

Trish sighed and poured herself a glassful, then sat down at the table. "What are you doing?"

"It's for my class. In case we have a test tonight." Her mother frowned and returned to her reading.

"Want me to quiz you?"

"Oh, would you do that?" Mrs. Masters' eyes lit up.

"Yeah, sure."

"Ask me questions from the parts I highlighted." Her mother handed her the book.

"Okay." Trish put down her apple, skimming the page. "Oooh, pink highlighter—that's nice." She grinned at her mother, then glanced back down at the page. "Uh, let's see. Henrik Ibsen is the father of—"

"Modern drama. Trish, you can do better than that," her mother said, clicking her tongue.

"Okay." Trish ran her finger down the page. "Hmmm. Ibsen's plays could be characterized as—"

"Problem plays." Her mother nodded.

"—taking a—"

"Realistic format."

"Right again." Trish searched for a more difficult question. "Ibsen's first play was—"

"*Catilina*, 1850."

"His final work was—"

"*When We Dead Awaken*, 1900."

"—which was about—"

"A sculptor, Rubek, who sacrifices his life to art at the expense of—"

Trish closed the book. "I wouldn't worry about the test too much."

"I guess I'm just not in the swing of the whole thing yet." Mrs. Masters patted their cat, Dumpling, who was rubbing against her leg, ready for dinner. "How'd math go?"

"Oh, that." Trish winced and gulped her orange juice. "I don't know, it was hard. Cosecant and all of that."

"What does cosecant mean?"

"One over sine theta."

"And what does that mean?" Her mother leaned forward, intrigued.

"I don't know," Trish admitted. "Something about circles. I don't really understand it."

"Maybe you ought to see about getting some extra help."

"I guess." Trish finished the orange juice. "Where's Greg?"

"In the den, supposedly folding towels. Why don't you go prod him along?"

"Okay." Trish put her glass in the sink and headed for the den.

Her little brother was slouched in an easy chair, watching a rerun of "The Brady Bunch," a basket of laundry next to him.

She gave him an impish hug from behind. "Dearest brother!"

"Come on, Trish, cut it out." He squirmed free. "That's gross."

"You mean you aren't going to give me a big hug because you're so happy to see me?" She sat down on the arm of the chair.

"Yuck." He shook her hand and looked back at the television.

"Come on," she said, moving to the love seat. "Help me with these towels."

"Gross." He took one out of the basket, staring at the television. "You know what? Jan's kind of pretty—for a girl."

Trish squinted at the screen. "How many times have you seen this one?"

"I don't know, six. It's the one where Peter's voice changes." He coughed experimentally. "Are you going to make fun of me when mine does?"

"Yup." She took two more towels from the basket.

They heard Freud barking as the front door slammed.

"Dad's home." Greg didn't turn from the television.

"Hi." Mr. Masters walked into the den, wearing a dark-gray business suit, a broad grin creasing his tennis-tanned face. "How are you two?"

"Fine," Trish answered for both of them. "Did you have a good day?"

"Sold six cars." His grin widened. "We're going to go ahead with the new branch in Cambridge." He ruffled her hair. "How'd the match go?"

She grinned back at him. "I won."

"How'd the team do?"

"We lost."

"One of these days you'll get them." He turned to Greg. "How about you?"

"School's gross," he said, not taking his eyes from the "Brady Bunch" credits. "Way to go with the cars."

"Yeah." Mr. Masters grabbed a towel and playfully wrapped it around his son's head, wrestling with him. "Where's your mother? I want to tell her."

"In the kitchen studying," Trish said.

"Think I'll interrupt her." He released Greg, who had been unsuccessfully struggling to get free.

"Dad, I could have gotten away!" he protested, flushed.

"I know." Mr. Masters smiled at him and headed for the kitchen. "Hey, Nancy, guess what?"

"He's in a good mood." Greg watched him go. "Bet he'll throw the football with me tonight." He scrambled out of his chair, chasing after his father. "Dad, you wanna play catch tonight?"

"What about the towels?" Trish asked, knowing that he

was already gone. With a resigned shrug, she took a few more out of the basket as the opening credits of "Gilligan's Island" flashed onto the screen.

"Hi, Trish." Rachael Needham, a thin black girl with tortoise-shell glasses and an easy smile, sat down next to her in homeroom the next morning. She was Trish's other best friend.

"Hi." Trish glanced up from her French homework.

"Recovered from the team's demoralizing loss?"

Trish nodded. "I'm being brave about it."

"Good girl," Rachael laughed. "How many seasons has it been since they've won?"

Trish shrugged. "I don't know, hundreds. Did you do your French?"

"Part of it." Rachael opened her book. "Only I didn't get the last two questions."

"Great." Trish surveyed her paper. "Neither did I. Oh, here," she said as their homeroom teacher, Mr. Bradford, called her name.

"Jake McDougal?" Mr. Bradford asked.

"Here," a boy said.

"Colin McNamara?" No one answered, and Mr. Bradford lifted his head, eyes irritated. "Anyone seen McNamara today?"

"He was down by the gym," a boy volunteered.

"I saw him too," a girl agreed.

The door opened and Colin sauntered in, casually arrogant in a blue-and-green flannel shirt and jeans, his hair rumpled.

"How goes it, teach?" he asked, both hands in his pockets.

Mr. Bradford's voice was very stiff. "McNamara, you're late."

"Only a couple minutes." Colin sat down in the back, swinging his feet up onto a desk. "How goes it, Nicky?" he asked the boy next to him.

"Not bad, Mac," the boy shrugged. "Beat up any old ladies this morning?"

"Hey, come on, it's early," Colin protested.

"You have a pass, McNamara?" Mr. Bradford asked. "Or an excuse?"

Colin checked all of his pockets.

"I know I had one," he said, then grinned. "Musta dropped it on the way down here."

"Well, suppose you go down to the office and get yourself another one." Mr. Bradford tightened an already tight tie.

"W-walk all the way down there alone?" Colin made his voice tremble. "P-please don't make me."

Most of the class laughed.

"What a jerk," Rachael muttered.

"Too bad he's good-looking," Trish agreed. "What a waste."

"I don't think he is." Rachael wrinkled up her nose. "He's too little."

"I don't think so. He just needs a haircut." Trish sat back, admiring his build in spite of herself.

"Look, I'm sick of it," Mr. Bradford was saying. "You pull this every day. Now get to the office!"

Colin gave him the tilted grin, pretending confusion.

"Move it!" Mr. Bradford ordered. "Or—"

The intercom clicked, and a sedate voice asked all homerooms to rise for the Pledge of Allegiance. Mr. Bradford motioned for everyone to stand up.

"That means you too, McNamara," he said.

"I'm sorry," Colin shrugged helplessly. "I'm a Communist."

Mr. Bradford scowled, but turned his attention to the flag. When the pledge was over, he turned back.

"Okay, McNamara, I'm not kidding," he said. "Get down to the office before I have them come drag you."

"Yes, sir! Thank you, sir!" Colin jumped up, snapping into a perfect military pose. He marched to the door, spinning around when he got to it with the authority of a general and scanning the room. Slowly, he nodded. "Very good, Bradford," he said crisply, his voice deep and commanding. "Shipshape. Carry on!" With a brief salute, he left.

Several people laughed, but sobered abruptly as Mr. Bradford remained silent at his desk.

"What a total jerk," Rachael muttered, frowning at the door.

Trish blushed, realizing that she'd been smiling. "Uh, yeah," she said, "he really is."

CHAPTER TWO

At lunch, Trish sat with Janet and Rachael near the end of a long table with the usual nucleus of people from their classes.

"This school is really boring," Rachael said, shaking her head. "Maybe I'll apply to Dartmouth next year; they have lots of guys there."

"My sister says that all Dartmouth guys do is road-trip," Janet disagreed.

Rachael laughed. "So, I'll go to Smith."

"Anyone want my dessert?" someone at the other end of the table asked. All the boys nearby immediately volunteered.

"Do you think the guys around here think the girls are really lousy?" Trish asked.

"Probably," Janet nodded, peeling an orange. "Besides, they're not *all* jerks."

Trish and Rachael automatically looked up the table where Peter Cameron, the tall, blond star of their French class, was sitting, arguing with another boy over the given-away bag of cookies.

Trish grinned. "Good old Peter."

"Pierre, Trish. Pierre," Rachael corrected her.

"Sorry. Pierre." Trish tried to give it the same French lilt. "*Il est extraordinaire.*"

"Anyway, *he's* not a jerk." Janet separated the orange segments. "Anyone want some?"

Trish accepted a piece. "Maybe at the next Student Council meeting, we can get everyone to have a Sadie Hawkins dance. Then you could ask him to it."

"Shh," Janet hissed, even though there was no way that Peter could have heard.

"I know who Trish would ask." Rachael took some of the rapidly disappearing orange. "Colin McNamara. In homeroom, she was talking about how cute he was."

"Yech," Janet said.

"Well, he is." Trish ducked as she managed to squirt orange juice at herself. "It's not that I like him or anything."

"God, I hope not." Janet shuddered. "He's so gross. You'll end up like—what was her name? The one he got pregnant."

"Diane something," Trish said. "But, I'm not planning on—"

"Good plan," Rachael nodded. "If you're going to get pregnant, try for better genes."

"Since when is she going to get pregnant?" Janet asked, a frown of confusion on her face.

Trish grinned. After all these years, Janet still didn't get Rachael's sense of humor. Actually, Trish didn't always get it either.

"Will you look at that guy?" Janet gestured toward the back of the noisy cafeteria, where Colin was wrestling with another boy as a teacher strode over to the scuffle, blowing his whistle. "You think he's ever *not* in trouble? I don't know why they don't just kick him out."

"He'll flunk out first. He can't even read." Rachael broke off part of the brownie someone had passed her and handed the rest to Trish. "You know who I'd ask, if they had a Sadie Hawkins? Mr. Caprio."

Mr. Caprio was the brawny basketball coach, blond and muscle-bound.

"And you're the one talking about taste?" Trish asked.

"Oh, come on, teach," Colin was saying as the teacher hustled him past. "We were just fooling around, we weren't mad or anything."

"Way to go, Mac!" a boy shouted. "You tell 'im!"

"Let's go, McNamara," the teacher said. "Why'd he say you jumped on him first?"

"I did. We were just kidding around."

The teacher nodded. "Right, McNamara, anything you say, McNamara."

"What a jerk," someone at Trish's table said.

"Someone should smash that twerp," a huge boy, obviously a football player, agreed.

"If you hurry, Trish," Rachael suggested cheerfully, "you could catch up and ask him about the dance."

"No, thanks." Trish shuddered. "I'd rather go with *Mr. Caprio.*"

"You and me both," Rachael said. "Wrestle you for him."

"No—thanks." Trish leaned forward, looking up the table. "Anyone want an apple?"

For the next few days, Trish forgot that Colin McNamara even existed, absorbed by tennis and the team's chance to possibly break its losing record in an upcoming match against Charleston High. Charleston was having a lot of flu. Trish was on her way out to practice with Janet and a few other people on the team when she realized that she'd left her wristband in her locker.

"Wait a minute," she said, stopping. "I have to go get my wristband. Tell Mrs. Jacobs I'll be right out."

A girl shook her head. "Boy, these temperamental players."

"I'll be right there." Trish broke into a jog down the hall toward the junior lockers.

"How goes it, kid?" Colin asked, passing her as she stretched to get the wristband from the top shelf of her locker.

"Fine." She kept stretching.

"You need help?" He extended his arm. "What do you want, this?" He took down the wristband.

"Yes," she said grudgingly. "Thank you."

He grinned at her.

"No problem, kid." He continued up the hall.

"I wish you'd stop calling me that," Trish said.

He turned. "Calling you what?"

"I'm not a kid—and I don't like people who are patronizing."

"Not a kid?" He ran his eyes up and down, pausing more than once, and Trish was suddenly humiliatingly aware that she was wearing shorts. "Yeah, guess you're right about that. Sorry." He winked and started up the hall again.

Flushed with both fury and embarrassment, Trish slammed her locker shut, trying to keep control. It didn't work and she spun around.

"You know, you're really a jerk!" she shouted after him. "I don't know if you think it makes people like you or what, but it doesn't! At least, not as far as I'm concerned. Can't you ever be nice to anyone?"

Eyebrows up, he turned.

"You talking to me?" he asked.

"What do you think? I think you're just a big, conceited jerk!" Trish put her hands on her hips.

He grinned slowly and moved down toward her.

"You really are a woman," he said. "My apologies."

"Well, you can keep them." She strode past him and down the hall, tightly gripping the wristband.

"You walk like a woman too!" he called after her.

She turned around, anger again overriding embarrassment.

"Why don't you just drop out or something, you know?" she asked.

"Or I could drop dead," he suggested. "Whichever you prefer."

"Why don't you do both!" She started up the hall again, late to practice.

Trish came home from practice in a terrible mood.

"Trish, is that you?" her mother called.

"Yeah." Trish dumped her books on the floor.

"How was school?"

"Rotten."

"How about practice?" Her mother came out into the hall, recognizing bad-mood symptoms.

"Lousy." Trish went past her into the kitchen, opened the refrigerator, and took out the orange juice. "I wish we'd get Tab, I hate this junk."

"And to think I've been waiting all day for my little bundle of sunshine to come home," Mrs. Masters said wryly.

Trish just grumbled.

Greg came in, scruffy in a worn sweatshirt and jeans, with Freud galloping behind him. He took the orange-juice carton from Trish, and gulped from the carton.

"Mom!" Trish wrenched it away from him.

"Greg, I don't want you doing that anymore, remember?" Mrs. Masters' voice was tired.

"Tattletale," Greg scowled.

Trish scowled back. "Stupid brat."

"Mom, Freud and me are gonna go play football with the guys." He headed for the door.

"Told you he was stupid," Trish said.

Mrs. Masters ignored that. "Where, Greg, in the Common?"

"Yeah. Be home in time for dinner." He got his football from the floor in the corner.

"What about unloading the dishwasher?" Mrs. Masters asked.

"It's Trish's turn."

"It is not." Trish pushed him. "I always do it."

"You're never even home." He pushed back. "I have to do all the work."

"You never do anything."

"Trish, unload the dishes." Mrs. Masters took her book and headed for the den. "And no more fighting about it."

"Yeah, so what if it's his turn," Trish muttered, throwing the dishwasher open and banging dishes onto the counter.

"Now you're mad," Greg said.

"I am not." She banged harder.

"Trish, could you maybe try not to break everything?" her mother called from the den.

Trish scowled and took out the next few dishes with exaggerated care.

"Yeah, well it *is* your turn," Greg said defensively.

"I know already, Greg! I'm doing it, okay?"

"Thought you said you weren't mad."

"Okay, so I'm mad!" Trish banged two plates. "I said it; are you satisfied?"

"Greg, why don't you go play football?" Mrs. Masters was back, very irritated. "And Trish, why don't you go somewhere too? I'll finish this up."

"I'm doing it already. God!" Trish dumped out the silverware. "Why's everyone bugging me?"

Mrs. Masters watched her for a minute as Greg escaped from the house with Freud and his football.

"When you're finished, Patricia," she said. "Maybe you feel like going on a walk."

"Maybe I don't," Trish said.

"Don't push me!" her mother advised.

Trish didn't say anything, but continued unloading, and her mother left the room. When she had finished with the dishes, Trish closed the machine and slouched into the den.

"I'm going to the library," she muttered.

Her mother didn't even look up. "Be back before dark. I don't like you walking around alone out there."

Trish nodded, leaving the room.

"Will you return the books on the front hall table?" her mother called after her.

"Yeah." Trish came back to the doorway, sensing that that might be the signal for a truce. "I'm sorry I grumped. I had a bad day."

"So I gathered," her mother said, still stiff.

"Yeah, well, sorry."

"Okay." Mrs. Masters broke into a smile. "Just come back in a more cheerful mood."

"Okay."

"And before dark."

"Okay."

Detention let out at four o'clock, and Colin walked slowly home. He had detention almost every afternoon. Today it was for being late to homeroom. Again. He slouched down Boylston Street, hands in his pockets, ignoring the people around him. Girls' tennis must have ended early today because the school courts had been empty when he passed. He loved to watch girls' tennis. Or was it Trish Masters he loved to watch?

He crossed the street to the Prudential Center, cutting through the chic shopping mall that included FAO Schwarz and Saks Fifth Avenue. The shortcut ended up on the second floor of the Sheraton Boston. He took the escalator down to the first floor, exiting through the main lobby of the hotel. His family's apartment was on Saint Germain Street, just beyond the hotel, in the shadow of the Christian Science buildings.

He let himself inside the apartment, then closed the door, straightening his slouch with an effort.

"Anyone here?" He made his voice sound cheerful.

When no one answered, he slumped again, moving to the kitchen. There was a note on the table in his mother's small handwriting.

Colin—had to run out to the store, back soon. Make sure you *eat* something. Love, Mom.

He put the note down and opened the refrigerator, staring inside it. Then he sighed and closed the door, heading out to the hall. His cat, Ophelia, was waiting for him; he carried her into his room, dropping a kiss on the little black-and-white head.

"How goes it, cat?" He sat down on the bed.

Ophelia purred, kneading her paws on his shirt.

"How come you like me, anyway?" he asked. "Don't you know I'm a big, conceited jerk?"

Ophelia purred.

Taking her with him, he lay down and stared up at the ceiling. He studied it for a minute, then looked around the room: at this morning's crumpled running clothes, the overcrowded bookshelves, the familiar posters, and, pausing longest, at the full-length Marilyn Monroe.

"Cheer me up, cat," he said. "Lousy day today."

Ophelia purred, rubbing her head against his.

"Colin?" His mother poked her head into the room and saw him lying down. "What's wrong? Are you sick?"

"I'm fine." He sat up hastily. "Hi."

She came all the way in. She was small with reddish-brown hair and Colin's deep-green eyes. She touched the back of her hand to his forehead, looking worried.

"I'm fine," he said.

"Hmmm." Not convinced, she took her hand off. Then her expression brightened. "I bought some nice ham. Why don't I make you a sandwich?"

"Thanks, but I'm not hungry."

"Look at you; you're bones. Come on."

"I'm really not hungry, Mom."

Still worried, she sat down next to him, hands folded in her lap.

"How was school today?" she asked.

"Okay."

"Did you learn a lot?"

"No."

She nodded, hands tightening.

"Sorry," he said. "Had kind of a lousy day, y'know?"

"Do you want to tell me about it?"

"No. Not really."

"Well, then." She thought for a minute, then straightened his limp flannel collar. "I know what would cheer you up. We'll go out and buy you some new clothes."

"What for?" He surveyed himself. "These're good enough."

"You wouldn't like some nice new shirts?"

"What for?"

"Because you're a looker," she shrugged, "and you walk around like—"

"Like what?" he asked stiffly.

His mother looked at him with familiar worried disappointment. His parents almost never got mad at him. Just disappointed.

"Come on," she said. "We'll get you some new things and the girls at school'll be all over you."

"Yeah, sure." He made his collar crooked again. "Look, Mom, thanks for, like, offering and everything, but I've got enough clothes."

"I just thought—"

He stood up. "Think I'll go get a sandwich."

"I'll make it for you." She got up too.

"Mom—"

"I want to. It makes me happy."

"Okay." He smiled. "I like the way you make them."

A few minutes later, he was sitting in the kitchen with his sandwich, giving small pieces of ham to Ophelia.

"Do you want some milk?" Mrs. McNamara offered him a glassful.

"No, thanks, I'm fine."

"Drink it, you need some meat on those bones."

He put a piece of ham on his shoulder and kept eating.

"How about some brownies?" she asked when he was finished.

"What, you running for Jewish Mother of the Year or something?"

"It just makes me happy to see you eat." She gave him a brownie.

He stuffed the whole thing into his mouth.

"There," he said with his mouth full. "I make your day?"

"Have another," she said.

He laughed, standing up.

"I'm going to the library," he said. "You want anything?"

"You just went."

"I'm done with 'em already. Thanks for the sandwich." He picked up Ophelia. "Come on, cat. Come help me find my books." He paused, grinning at his mother. "Maybe you ought to pack me some provisions for the hike to my room."

CHAPTER THREE

Trish meandered through the Boston Public Library. She didn't like using the little memory-bank computers the library had instead of a card catalog, so she usually just wandered around, picking up books that looked interesting. For a minute, she watched a man reading a book upside down; then, realizing it was probably getting late, she walked toward the main staircase. Hurrying, she almost bumped into someone.

"Excuse me—" She stopped and stared, recognizing Colin.

As he saw her, he stiffened.

"What are you doing here?" he demanded.

"Uh, well." Trish frowned at her books. "The same thing you are, I guess."

He ran his free hand through his hair, unmistakably rattled.

"Sports," he said. "I like to read about sports."

"Which ones?"

"I don't know. You know." He backed up toward the stone railing, dropping two of the books when he hit it sooner than he expected.

"*The Old Man and the Sea?*" Trish asked, bending to pick one up.

He got to it first. "Fishing."

"How about *Richard the Second?*" She picked up the other one.

"Uh, murder."

She gave it to him. "What are you, a brain?"

"I gotta go, I'm late." He turned, walking swiftly down the stairs.

Trish watched him go, confused.

"Hey!" He was suddenly back. "Hey, woman!"

She looked at him uncertainly.

"It's getting dark outside." His voice was accusing.

"Oh?" She tilted her head, not sure what he meant.

"You walk around in the dark every night?"

"I only live a couple of blocks away."

"So you walk around in the dark? You know how stupid that is?"

"No," she said, grinning. "I'm not a brain."

"Yeah, well, how long you gonna be in here?"

"I don't know, I guess—"

"Well, I'll wait," he grumbled. "Don't feel like reading about you in *The Globe* tomorrow."

"You don't have to—"

"I said I was waiting already."

"Um, I guess I can go now." Trish started down the stairs.

He nodded, indicating that he'd be by the door.

"You really don't have to do this," Trish said once they were outside. "I can walk by myself; I do it all the time."

"Terrific, you do it all the time." He shook his head.

Neither spoke for a minute.

"Which way?" he asked.

"It's not far—I live on Commonwealth."

He nodded, one hand stuffed in his pocket.

"Hey, uh." He kept his eyes ahead. "I'm sorry."

"About what?"

"You know what." He hunched his shoulders, the wind picking up as they rounded the corner. "Guess I am kind of a jerk."

"No, I—"

"Don't bother, okay?"

"Well, I'm sorry too. I didn't mean to get so mad."

"*You* would have been a jerk if you hadn't."

They crossed the street.

"Do you mind if people call you Colin?" she asked.

"What do you mean, mind?"

"Well, they all call you Mac."

"Kind of bugs me. I like Colin."

"Okay—Colin."

"Right." He smiled briefly. "You get bugged when people call you 'woman'?"

"It's better than 'kid.' "

Their eyes met for a second and he looked away.

"Uh, we turn up here," she said.

"Didn't know you were rich." He looked up at the town houses, windows starting to fill with warm lights.

"We're not."

"Right."

They were both silent again.

"I-it's up there." Trish pointed, starting across the street.

"Hey, watch it!" He yanked her back out of the way of all the cars. "God, don't you look?"

"I'm sorry," she said with automatic guilt. Lots of times, she forgot to look.

"Well, that's about the stupidest thing you can do." He scowled, then released her arm a little late. "Where'd you say your house was?"

She pointed again, not moving from the curb. He looked to see if any cars were coming, then crossed with her to the grassy mall running down the middle of the street.

"This is it," she said unnecessarily when they'd reached the other side.

"Right," he nodded. "It's nice."

"Oh. Thank you." She shifted her books to her other arm. "Thank you for walking me. You really didn't have to. . . ."

"Don't walk around in the dark, woman," he said, shrugging. "I'd better get going. Later."

Trish nodded. "Right."

As she stepped into the front hall, her mother was out of the living room to meet her, hands on her hips. "What was the last thing I said to you?" she wanted to know.

"Be home before dark."

"Well, don't you think you could have managed? I wasn't kidding about not liking you out alone. You're sixteen years old, Patricia; I really shouldn't have to be reminding you about these things."

"I'm sorry," Trish said guiltily. "Anyway, I'm not that stupid. A guy walked me home."

"Oh, even better. Now you're picking up men at the city library!" Mrs. Masters threw up her arms as if all hope were lost.

"I know him from school."

"Oh." Her mother's expression relaxed a little. "Is he a friend of yours?"

"I don't know," Trish said.

"Guess what?" Janet said as she hit a backhand volley at practice a few days later.

"What?" Trish asked, up at the net next to her.

"I saw *him* after school."

"The great Pierre?" Trish knocked a shot crosscourt. "Tell all."

"We're going out Friday."

"Yeah, really?" Trish looked over, lowering her racket. "That's really good. Whose idea was it?"

"Come on, you two," their coach called from another court. "Big match tomorrow."

Trish resumed the ready position.

"Whose idea was it?" she asked more quietly.

"He said, '*The Graduate* is one of the Harvard Square movies this Friday.' And I said, 'Oh, I love that movie, don't you?' And he said, 'Why don't we go? I mean, if you want to.' And I said, 'I'd love to,' and so, we're going." Janet's shot hit the tape and fell back down.

"Not bad." Trish flipped the ball to the other side. "I wish I had a love life."

"I don't have a love life." Janet stretched for a high one.

28

"Yet," Trish said. "Did you hear Gail and Chuck broke up?"

"Again? I bet they end up married."

"I bet they end up divorced." Trish's shot went out-of-bounds.

"Is it my imagination or did you two just ask me if you could run some laps?" Mrs. Jacobs, their coach, called.

Janet bent for a low forehand. "I think it was your imagination."

"Mmmm." Mrs. Jacobs smiled and came over to their court, leaning against the netpost. "Heidi, Lois, you two come up, and Janet and Trish, you hit net shots to them. Wouldn't it be great if we won tomorrow?"

After they hit for a while, Mrs. Jacobs nodded.

"Okay, Janet, Trish, you two take some more volleys. In about ten minutes, we'll get some matches going." She moved onto another court.

"Are you going to that drama meeting tonight?" Janet asked.

"Yeah, probably," Trish said, concentrating on her shots. "Aren't we *finally* talking about what play we want to do?"

"So you hear. I think I can get the car." Janet sighed, frustrated, as her shot ticked the tape again. "You know, the PSATs are coming up."

"I bet you bought one of those books."

"Well, yeah," Janet admitted.

"I figured." Trish grinned. "Bet you've been practicing too."

"Well, yeah, a little."

"I figured."

Janet grinned back. "I hope you're still laughing when I'm at Yale and you're off in Iowa somewhere."

"What's wrong with Iowa?"

"I don't know," Janet turned just in time to hit the ball. "Just one of those places."

"You'll probably get into Yale."

Janet hit another into the net.

"Probably on a tennis scholarship," she agreed.

"Probably." Trish hit one into the net too.

"Yech, we have an audience."

"So, show off." Trish threw the two balls over the net.

"In front of him? Yech."

"Who is it?" Trish sliced a volley crosscourt, bouncing on the balls of her feet to be ready for the next shot.

"Colin McNamara."

Trish hit the ball into the net. Embarrassed, she turned enough to see him leaning up against a car, staring toward the courts.

"Trish!" Heidi shouted, and Trish ducked instinctively, the ball glancing off her shoulder.

"Keep your mind on the game," Mrs. Jacobs said.

"Sorry." Trish tried to concentrate but, self-conscious about her movements, missed the next ball completely.

"Where's your form?" Mrs. Jacobs asked. "Keep your eye on the ball."

"You know what I think?" Janet had been hitting with boring regularity.

"What do you think?" Trish stroked the next one into the net. She glanced over and saw, thankfully, that he was gone. Relaxing, she slammed the ball perfectly crosscourt.

"I think you like him."

"I think you're crazy."

Taking her time, Trish was the last one out of the locker room after practice. Janet had accepted a ride home. Trish felt like walking.

"Have a nice night," the janitor, who had been waiting patiently to get in and clean, said as she passed him coming out. "You the last one?"

"Yeah," she nodded. "Sorry. See you later, Mr. Reynolds." She glanced up ahead and saw Colin coming down the hall.

"Hey, woman." His voice was casual. "What are you doing around here this late?"

"Tennis practice."

"Yeah? I didn't know you were—" He stopped. "Well, that is . . ."

She rescued him. "What are you doing around here?"

"You know." He shrugged, holding the door for her. "Which way you heading?"

"Home, I guess."

"I'm going down that way." He looked at her books. "Your stuff heavy?"

"No, thanks, I've got it."

"Rough practice?" he asked as they crossed the almost empty parking lot. "You look kind of tired."

Trish sighed. "Aggravating practice."

"How many matches you have left?"

"Four."

"What's your record?"

"Depressing."

"Well, you're good, aren't you?"

"Not really." She thought about all the shots she'd missed that day.

"Aren't you like, second singles?"

"Well, yeah," she admitted. "Sort of."

"You must be good, then."

"Not really. Do you play?"

"I have." They stopped at the curb as the "Don't Walk" sign flashed. "It's not my thing, though."

"What is your thing?"

"Dunno." His hands went into his pockets. "Guess I get into running."

"You mean, like miles?"

"More fun that way." He took a leaflet from an earnest young promotion man in front of a record store. "You wanna buy a stereo cheap?"

"No, thank you."

"Too bad." He crumpled the paper and flipped it into a trash can.

"How many miles?"

"What, to your house? It's only a few blocks."

"I mean, how many miles do you run," Trish laughed.

"Three, sometimes four. Once six. It's pretty fun."

"I never do it," Trish said, shaking her head. "I get bored."

"Learn to talk to yourself."

"I guess." She switched her books to her other arm, moving her tennis racket to her free hand.

"You sure those aren't too heavy?"

She nodded. "Oh, yeah. One good thing about math is that the book's usually pretty small."

"That's the only good thing about math," he said wryly.

"That's for sure." Trish made a motion as though to throw her Trig book into the trash can they were passing on the crowded street. "Which one are you taking?"

"Huh?" He apparently didn't hear her.

Trish didn't say anything, relieved that they were turning toward Commonwealth and she was almost home.

"It really is nice around here," he said as they walked down the grassy mall. "If I had a dog, I'd bring it here every day."

"We've got a dog."

"Yeah? What's its name?"

"Freud."

"He preoccupied with sex?" Colin tilted his head, amused.

"Latency period," Trish said solemnly.

"We've got a cat—kind of dumb, but she's cute. Call her Ophelia—she gets into water." His expression was very serious. "She knows what she is, but not what she may be."

"Wow." Trish stared at him, impressed. "Can you do that for the whole play?"

"Huh?" His hand went through his hair. "I don't know."

"Ophelia says that, right?"

"I don't know." He shifted his shoulders, uncomfortable. "You have any cats?"

32

"One. His name's Dumpling—he fell into the batter when he was a kitten, and we couldn't resist."

"Did you eat the dumplings?"

"They were delicious."

He grinned, shaking his head. "I bet." He glanced at her, then focused on scuffed running sneakers. "Uh, Trish?"

"What?"

"You get into movies?"

Trish thought about Janet suddenly.

"Yeah," she said. "Do you?"

"You go to a lot?"

"All the time."

"Uh," he stared even harder at his sneakers. "You think you sort of maybe might want to go to one Friday night?"

"I'd love to."

"Really?" His head snapped up. "You don't think I'm a jerk?"

Trish blushed. "No."

"Wow." He stopped, noticing that they were in front of her house. "Um, well—" his hand went through his hair again—"yeah, uh, let's see. What if I came by like around seven or something?"

She smiled at him. "Sounds great."

"Yeah? Well, uh, okay, then." He backed up toward the street. "Then, I guess I'll see you then. Uh, bye."

"Bye."

He turned, bumping into a streetlight.

"Excuse me," he said absently.

Trish watched him go, then let herself into the house, taking the front steps two at a time, dropping her books and racket in the general vicinity of the hall table.

"Hey," she shouted. "Guess what!"

CHAPTER FOUR

It was just before seven, Friday night, and Trish was in her room, getting ready. She heard the front doorbell ring and froze. A minute later, Greg came pounding up the stairs.

"He's here!" he tried to whisper, unsuccessfully.

"Really?" Trish swallowed. "Where is he? Talking to Mom and Dad?"

"Yeah."

Brush in hand, she frowned at the mirror.

"Do I look all right?" she asked.

"Yeah, sure." He studied her for a second, then nodded. "Even kind of pretty."

"Thanks." Trish gave up and dropped the brush.

"Have fun."

"Thanks." She glanced in the mirror and got scared again.

Colin was in the living room, perched on the couch, wearing gray pants and a green V-neck sweater with a white shirt poking out. He stood up nervously when she came in; his arms hung awkwardly, hands wanting to go into his pockets, not sure what to do.

"Hi," he said weakly.

"Hi." Trish's voice was just as weak as she stared at this neatly dressed boy; only the unruly dark hair seemed familiar. "I, uh, I guess you've met my parents."

"Yeah."

No one said anything for a minute.

"Maybe you two ought to get going if you want to make a movie," Mr. Masters suggested.

"I guess we should." Colin nodded. "Um, it's very nice to have met you, Mr. and Mrs. Masters."

Trish's mother smiled. "You too, Colin."

"We won't be late," he assured her. He glanced at Trish. "Do you wear a coat or anything like that?"

"Oh, right." Trish hurried to the front hall closet to get a blazer, followed by both her parents and Colin. "I guess we'll see you later."

"Have fun," Mr. Masters said.

Trish looked at her mother, who mouthed the word "Relax."

"Bye," Trish said.

"Nice to have met you," Colin said.

"You sure you'll be warm enough?" he asked, once they were outside.

"I'm fine," she said, nodding.

"You look nice."

"Thank you. You do too."

They both smiled tightly.

"So, uh, what movie you want to see?" he asked.

"Whatever you want."

"It's up to you. There's that German thing, the one about ax murders, Woody Allen's new thing—all kinds of stuff."

"I don't like ax murders that much," Trish admitted.

"Do you speak German?"

"No."

"You like Woody Allen?"

"Yes."

"Let's go."

At the cinema ticket booth, Trish reached a hesitant hand into her pocket for money, not sure if he was going to pay.

He pulled his wallet out of his back pocket. "Put it away."

"Well . . ."

"Put it away."

Slowly, she shoved the money back.

"You want popcorn or anything?" he asked.

"Whatever you want."

"Not that again." He shook his head. "Do you like popcorn?"

"Yes."

"Okay." He turned to the bored older man behind the candy cases. "Could we have a medium popcorn, please?"

The theater was very large, and what might have been a sizable crowd in an average cinema, here looked completely lost. Rows of empty red seats spread out in front of them.

"Well." Trish took off her blazer, folding it over her arm.

"Hmmm," he agreed. Then he strode down the aisle, stopping a few rows past the halfway mark, stepping back to let her go in first. He sat down next to her, handing her the popcorn as the lights went down.

"Just in time," he whispered.

"Yeah, really," Trish whispered back. "I thought they might hold the show until a few hundred other people showed up."

As the movie began, she found herself particularly aware of him sitting next to her. She threw him several quick, darting glances, trying to see what he was doing, trying not to be obvious about it. She lifted the bucket of popcorn onto the arm of the chair between them.

"I don't want to sit here and eat it all," she explained.

He took a handful. "You never would have pulled it off."

Trish returned her gaze to the movie.

What was it about sitting next to a male that was so overpowering? Why did the air seem thicker? Was it aftershave? Was he wearing after-shave? Mmmm, he definitely was. She wondered what kind.

Woody Allen, your favorite, she reminded herself. So, you're sitting next to a boy at a movie; don't make such a big thing about it. But what was he thinking about? Probably the movie, she told herself, that's why we're here—sort of. What could be worse than a first date? No date at all. Watch the movie.

He really was cute, though. He had such nice shoulders, nothing bulky about them. Long, supple arms—watch the movie.

She heard the people around her laugh at something one of the characters had said, and joined in, a little late.

She had finally allowed herself to be drawn into the movie when she caught a slight movement to her left. She glanced over and saw his tentatively creeping right hand yank itself back down. Quickly, she turned back to the screen, embarrassed.

Again there was a flash of movement, and again she involuntarily looked over. This time, his uplifted hand snaked over to his shirt, as if he were straightening his collar. Flushing, she stared at the screen.

Leaning forward as the plot intensified, she didn't notice his arm slide over, getting the seat. She sat back, running into it as he was pulling away, and they both froze, embarrassed.

"Uh, sorry." He kept his arm there.

"No, I'm sorry." Forgetting about the popcorn, she put her elbow onto the arm of the chair, knocking the bucket into his lap. "Colin, I'm sorry, I—"

"Don't worry, it's not buttered." He brushed the kernels off. He looked at her, then withdrew his arm, and with one quick motion flipped the entire bucket up so that it landed with a dull cardboard thud two rows in front of them.

Several people turned to stare, and Colin shrugged benignly.

"Feel better now?" he asked.

She nodded. "Much."

"Good." He settled his arm around her shoulders, and she leaned back against the warmth to enjoy the movie.

"That was good," he laughed when the lights came back on. Flustered, he withdrew his arm. "I mean, did you like it?"

"Very much." Trish took her blazer from the seat next to her.

"Oh, let me help you." Awkwardly, he guided her arms through the sleeves. "Why don't we go this way?" he pointed to her side of the row. "It's still pretty early. You want to get something to eat?"

"Sure."

Out on the sidewalk, she caught sight of a small, somewhat dingy restaurant called Ray's that was still open.

She pointed. "How about there?"

"Yeah, I guess." He hesitated, not crossing right away.

"What's wrong?" She looked at the approaching traffic. "They aren't that close."

"Sometimes you can't tell when they have headlights on." He coughed. "Sorry, I guess I get kind of cautious."

"It's a good way to be. My mother's always yelling at me for forgetting to look."

"You should listen to her."

"Yeah, I should." She glanced at him after the cars had passed, he nodded, and they crossed the street.

Inside the restaurant, they sat at a small table by the wall. A squat waitress bustled over with menus.

"Ready to order?" She whipped out her pad.

Trish skimmed the menu.

"I'll have a salad," she said. "With French dressing, please."

"Salad?" Colin raised his eyebrows. "You don't have to have *salad*."

"I like salad."

"Oh." He looked back at his menu. "I guess I'll have a, I don't know, roast-beef sandwich and a Coke. What do you want to drink, Trish?"

"Tab, please."

"Tab?" He put down his menu. "What, are you on a diet or something? God, you're bones." He flushed at this echoing of his mother, closing his eyes for a second.

"I like Tab," Trish said simply.

"She likes Tab." He gave the waitress the two menus and she clumped away on sensible oxfords.

"So." Colin cleared his throat.

"I enjoyed the movie."

"Me too," he agreed. "Yeah, good movie." Nervously, he moved his hand forward to play with the salt shaker, but knocked it over. He winced, then picked it up and tossed some salt over his shoulder.

"Superstitious?" Trish asked.

"What? Oh, guess I'm in the habit. My mother—she's doing that stuff all the time. You know."

"Like knocking on wood?"

"Yeah. And if you drop a knife, a man's coming to visit."

"Really?" Trish looked down at her silverware. "What if I dropped my fork?"

"A woman."

"How about my spoon? There's nothing left."

"It means a kid's coming. Least, that's what my mother says. Like Dad dropped a spoon the other night and some friend of hers called after dinner and said she was pregnant. My mother got all excited—kept shouting 'See? See?' all night."

"Do you have any brothers and sisters?"

"No, just me." He grinned wryly. "After I showed up, they were afraid to try again."

"The only child. You must be spoiled."

"They let me get away with murder," he agreed. "Oh, thanks," he said as the waitress put down his sandwich.

"Thank you," Trish echoed him as she got her salad.

"Salad, huh?" He shook his head. "You should have gotten something decent."

"I like salad." She picked up the little cup of dressing. "Before I do this, do you like olives?"

"Yeah, sure."

"Here." She transferred them to his plate. "Tell me three other things you like."

"What?"

"I don't know, three things you like."

"You've been reading *Seventeen*, huh?" he asked.

She flushed. "So, what if I have?"

"I knew it." He took a gulp of Coke.

"So, tell me three things."

"I don't want to play."

"It's not a game," she said. "I'm serious."

"Okay, Big Macs. I like Big Macs. Can we quit now?"

"Boy, you're a lot of fun."

"Okay, I like running."

"I already knew that." She tried to spear a cherry tomato and missed. "What's your favorite book?"

"I don't know how to read," he said stiffly.

"Then, how come you were in the library?"

"I look at the pictures."

"In Hemingway?"

He scowled, putting his sandwich down.

"Can we talk about something else?" he asked.

"No."

"Guess your friends thought it was pretty funny, you seeing me in the library," he scowled.

"I didn't mention it. I thought it might embarrass you."

"You thought right." He gulped down most of the Coke.

"Come on, Colin. I'm not going to make fun of you or anything."

"Okay, *Farewell to Arms*," he said, scowling harder. "Now, can we shut up about it?"

She nodded silently.

"Oh, terrific." He shoved his plate away. "Now you're mad."

"I'm not mad." She kept her eyes on her salad, playing with the lettuce. "You just sort of hurt my feelings."

"Oh, great—guilt. Now I'm supposed to apologize."

"Do what you want, Colin." Her voice was very quiet.

Neither spoke for a long minute.

" 'They have tied me to a stake,' " he said finally. " 'I cannot fly. But, bearlike, I must fight the course.' "

She looked up. "What?"

"*Macbeth*." He smiled slightly. "Act Five."

"And you're flunking out," she said.

"Yup." He picked up his sandwich.

"Is it none of my business?"

"I'm flunking out because I'm stupid."

"But you're not."

"Yeah, I am. Look at the classes I'm taking—shop, stupid Functional Math, Spanish One. . . ."

"What's wrong with that?"

"Hey, don't bother, okay?" His voice was irritated. "I know they're stupid classes. Hey, I'm not even in a real English class, I'm in Remedial Reading. My science class is horticulture—what are you in, chemistry? Something like that? What do you mean, I'm not stupid?" His voice was rising and he glanced around to see if anyone had noticed. "You know what happens if I give an answer in one of my classes?" He spoke more calmly. "The teacher nods and says, 'Very good, Colin. Good job.' They even speak slowly to make sure I understand! And you say I'm not stupid." He took a vicious bite of his sandwich.

"What are you getting in reading?"

"I don't know, a D? Something like that."

"Sort of fulfilling their expectations?"

"Yup." He gulped some Coke. "They want me to be dumb, I'll be dumb."

Trish moved lettuce idly in her bowl.

"You know what you are?" she asked.

"Come on, Trish, I get this all the time."

"You're a closet intellectual, that's what you are."

He laughed, the irritation slipping away.

"Is that what you think?" he asked.

"That's exactly what I think."

"You're cute, you know that?" He grinned at her. "And even cuter when you blush." He reached over, touching her hand. "Trish—"

"Kids?" the waitress asked. "I hate to do this to you, but we're kind of closing up and—"

"Oh, sorry." Colin took one last bite of his sandwich,

fishing for his wallet. By the time he'd paid and they were outside, he'd managed to change the subject to the movie, which they talked about until they got to her house.

He glanced at his watch. "Good, it's not too late." He gestured toward the lights coming from the living room. "Your parents still up?"

"Looks like it," Trish said nodding. "Thank you, I had a nice time."

"You don't have to be polite."

"I'm not. I had a good time."

"I'm sorry I lost my temper."

"It's okay."

"Not really," he said.

They were both silent.

"Well, it's—it's getting kind of late." Trish backed up a step.

"Yeah, it is." He swallowed. "Guess I'd better get going."

"Yeah, me too."

"Yeah." He leaned forward and his lips brushed across hers. "Uh—goodnight."

"Goodnight."

As he went briskly down the walk, she started up the front steps.

"Colin?" she asked, turning.

He pulled his hands out of his pockets. "What?"

"You said you wished you had a dog you could walk." She held on to the cast-iron railing, not sure if she was going too far. "If it's nice tomorrow, do you maybe feel like walking a lazy basset hound with a lot of sexual hangups?"

His grin came so fast that she could see the sudden white of his teeth in the darkness.

"Yeah," he said. "Sounds good."

CHAPTER FIVE

"Hi." Trish wandered into the den, where her parents were watching television.

"Oh, good," her mother said, looking up. "Did you have a nice time?"

"Yeah." She sat down on her father's other side.

"I feel so old." He gave her a one-armed hug. "My little girl going out on dates."

Trish turned so she could see both of them. "Did you like him?" she asked.

"He seems very nice," her mother said. "Poor thing, he was scared to death. You two don't know each other very well, do you?"

"Better now," Trish shrugged. "He's coming over tomorrow and we're going to take Freud for a walk."

"Romantic," her father said.

"Yeah," Trish agreed. She stood up, smiling. "Yeah, it was fun. Think I'll go up and get ready for bed."

"How was the movie?" her mother asked.

"What movie?" Trish picked up Dumpling, who yawned sleepily and flopped in her arms.

"When'd she get so pretty?" Mr. Masters asked, watching her go.

Getting home, Colin found his mother in the living room watching the "Tonight Show," Ophelia on her lap. He sat down next to them. Ophelia moved over to greet him, purring deep in her throat.

He stroked his cat under the chin. "Thought Dad got off at midnight."

"They broke up a drug ring, and he had to stay late to fill

out reports." She smiled at him. "Did you have a nice time?"

"Yeah."

"You're home early."

"Her parents wanted her to be."

"But you had a good time?"

"Yeah."

Feeling ignored, Ophelia climbed onto his lap, and butted her head against his chest.

He patted her. "Sorry, kid."

"You look so handsome tonight." Mrs. McNamara tried to straighten his hair. "Just doesn't want to stay in place, does it?"

"No." Automatically, he patted it down.

"But such a nice wave to it. I bet this girl thinks you're a looker."

"Doubt it," he said. "Cat, what's this tail doing in my face?"

Ophelia purred, burrowing her head in his sweater.

Mrs. McNamara laughed. "That animal adores you."

"She has lousy taste."

"Just like this girl, right?"

Colin shrugged.

"So, what's she like?"

He shrugged again. "You know."

"Like Diane?" she asked casually.

"No."

"Blond?"

"Well, yeah," he grinned. "She's cute." Still grinning, he flipped Ophelia over and started rubbing her stomach while she purred blissfully. He glanced up and saw his mother's worried expression. "She's not like Diane, okay, Mom? Christ, she gets all A's."

"Colin."

"Sorry. I mean, *goodness,* she gets all A's."

"Really?" Interested now, his mother reached forward and turned the television off.

"Yeah. She's on student council and junk. Doesn't cake on makeup or anything—you'd like her."

"She sounds wonderful. I hope I get to meet her."

"Maybe." Absentmindedly, he pushed back on one of Ophelia's front paws as she playfully swatted at him. "I don't think it'll last."

"Why not?"

"I don't know, she's a brain. Gets along with her teachers, probably wants to go to Harvard—it's not going to work out."

"But you can do so many things, Colin. You just—" She stopped, frowning down at her hands.

"Just what?"

"You just won't. Your teachers call and tell me you can't read, and won't go to your tutors, and I keep telling them you read all the time, and they show me results of tests that say . . . I don't know. I just wish you could—"

"Come on, cat, you're annoying me." Colin winced as Ophelia swatted him again, still lying on her back. He shook his head, rubbing her stomach. "Y'ever get the feeling she's giggling at us?"

"Colin, can't we ever talk?"

"We are talking."

His mother just looked at him.

"Come on, Mom." He shifted his position; Ophelia shifted in response. "Do we have to get into it? Let's watch the 'Tonight Show.' "

"It's over."

"So, let's watch the 'Tomorrow Show.' "

"Colin."

"Look," he said, standing, and lifting Ophelia up with him. "Maybe I should just go to bed."

"Okay." She picked up a copy of *Time*.

He looked at her for a minute, feeling guilty.

"When's Dad gonna be home?"

"He wasn't sure."

"Well, maybe I'll wait a little while." He sat down again.

"If you want to watch 'Tomorrow,' you can."

He shrugged and flipped it on just in time for them to hear the host announce that this show would be spent discussing dyslexia.

"Sometimes in reading, I walk around backwards," he said. "Just to freak her out, y'know?"

"That's not funny."

"I guess not," he agreed.

For a few minutes, neither spoke; Colin patted his cat, Mrs. McNamara leafed through a magazine.

"Guess it would be easier on you and Dad if I *did* have dyslexia," he said quietly.

"Of course it wouldn't! How can you say such a thing?" His mother stared at him.

"You guys must be pretty ashamed of me."

"You're our son; of course we're not ashamed of you."

"But you're not proud."

"Of course we're proud. You're our son."

"But you're not," he shook his head. "How could you be? I get in trouble, I'm like, flunking out—what's to be proud of? I mean, okay, I'm your son, but you can't tell people about me and how proud you are."

"Colin . . ."

"When you introduce me, you always say, 'Doesn't he cut a fine figure of a man?' But you can't say things and be proud. You can't tell them about my varsity letters, or the honor roll, or—what's to say, 'the kid's cat likes him'?"

"I don't know what you're talking about," Mrs. McNamara said, her magazine forgotten.

"It was just tonight." He slumped down, letting Ophelia rub her head against his chin.

"What did that girl say to you?" His mother was getting angry. "She sounds awful."

"It wasn't her, she didn't do anything. It was just her parents." He let out his breath. "I saw this huge trophy on a shelf, and they were so proud, they told me it was Trish's, she won it in a tennis tournament. They were really nice—asked me what I liked to do, what I wanted to be—and I felt like a jerk. They must have thought I was really stupid. I know *she* does. I just—'' He expelled his breath in a sharp burst. "Forget it, I'm sorry. Can we not talk about this anymore?"

"Colin—"

"I really don't want to. I'm just sorry you and Dad—let's watch something else, huh?" He was up and changing the channels. "Oh, wow, Fred Astaire, you want to watch Fred Astaire? Yeah, let's watch it." He sat down, pulling Ophelia back onto his lap.

"Are you sure you don't want to talk?" His mother touched his shoulder.

"Real sure."

"Well, you know how much your father and I—"

"Please, Mom? Can we please not?"

She looked at him for a second, then nodded.

"Okay," she said.

The next day, it rained.

Trish leaned against one of the windowsills in the living room scowling, as her mother sat on the couch writing letters.

"Patricia, did I ever tell you that you brighten up my day?" Mrs. Masters asked. "Oh, the second I woke up this morning and saw the rain, and knew how you were going to react—let me tell you, it was a magical moment."

"It's not funny." Trish rested her chin in her hands, elbows on the sill. "Everything's ruined."

"Oh, I don't think it's so bad," Mrs. Masters said. "The crops needed it."

Trish had to laugh. "Come on, Mom, I'm not kidding. You're supposed to be comforting me."

"A child who goes to pieces over a little rain is beyond saving."

"Well, what do I do? Should I call him? Or wait? Or what?"

"You should relax." Her mother kept writing. "Nothing's ruined. Maybe you two can go over to the art museum."

"Oh, yeah." Trish rolled her eyes. "Sounds like fun."

"He seems like an intelligent boy. Did you meet him in one of your classes?"

"Well, not really," Trish said, a little embarrassed.

The phone rang and she jumped. "Oh, no, what if it's him?"

"Isn't that what you want?"

"I don't know."

"Trish?" Greg bellowed from upstairs. "Telephone! It's a guy! Come quick before he hangs up!"

Trish looked at her mother.

"Do I have permission to hit him?" she asked.

"Yes."

"Thanks." Trish went into the kitchen and picked up the phone. "Hello?"

"Oh, sorry, I was just hanging up." Colin paused. "It's me."

"Yeah, hi."

"Hi. Uh, how are you?"

"Fine. How are you?"

"Fine. It's, uh," he cleared his throat, "raining."

"I know."

"Well. Do you melt?"

"Not usually."

"I kind of get into rain. Feel like going anyway?"

"I'd love to."

"Your dog mind getting wet?"

"I don't know, I'll check with him." Trish glanced under the kitchen table where Freud was on his back, asleep.

"It's okay then if I come down in a while?"

"Oh, yeah, definitely."

"Okay. Then, I'll—I'll see you then."

"Okay." Trish hung up.

"Who was that?" her mother asked as Trish came through the living room, grinning.

"Obscene phone call," Trish said, shrugging.

Her mother nodded. "They always cheer me up too."

When the doorbell rang twenty minutes later, Mr. Masters, momentarily dislodged from the Red Sox, answered it.

Colin stood there, dripping wet. "Hi, Mr. Masters," he said, grinning sheepishly. "Is Trish around?"

"Sure, come on in." Mr. Masters opened the door all the way. "Really coming down out there, isn't it?"

"Yeah." He stepped tentatively into the hall. "Would it be better if I stayed outside?"

"Of course not." Mr. Masters moved to the stairs. "Trish? Colin's here! Colin, really, come in. It's only water."

"I guess. What's the score?" Colin gestured toward the sound of the television.

"Two all, top of the third."

"Not raining there, I bet," Colin said wryly, staying by the door.

"Hi." Trish bounced down the stairs. "Oh, wow. You want me to get you a towel or something?"

"No, you don't have to—"

"Be right back." She headed up the stairs, returning a few seconds later with a thick, green towel.

Colin took it uncertainly. "But this is so nice."

"No, we use it for Freud," Mr. Masters assured him.

Just putting the towel to his hair, Colin stiffened, but recovered himself and rubbed his hair vigorously.

"He was kidding," Trish said.

Colin grinned from underneath the towel, but didn't say anything.

"Hey, Freud?" Trish called.

Freud dashed out from the kitchen, his tail whipping back and forth.

"Want to go on a walk?" She got the leash out of the closet.

He scratched at the door, panting.

"Oh, hi, Colin," Mrs. Masters said, coming downstairs. "I thought that was the door."

"Hello, Mrs. Masters." Colin lowered the towel, his hair spiky and bedraggled. "I'm sorry I got this wet."

"No problem; we use it for Dumpling," she said, looking a little confused when she got a bigger laugh than she'd expected.

Outside, Trish pulled up the hood of her slicker.

"Maybe Mom was right and we should have brought an umbrella," she said.

"Oh, I like it," Colin shrugged, as they crossed to the walkway, very deserted for a Saturday afternoon. Then he looked guilty. "I'm sorry, maybe we should go back. You might catch cold or something."

"Don't worry, I'll melt first."

"Terrific." He glanced up, the rain plastering his hair back against his forehead. "Pretty wet."

"That's for sure."

"This is pretty stupid."

"Yeah," she agreed cheerfully. "Where you want to go?"

"I don't know, Public Gardens?"

"Sure."

They walked down Commonwealth toward Arlington Street, both hunching their shoulders against the torrent, Freud so overjoyed to be going on a walk that he didn't even seem to notice.

"Boy, this is pretty stupid," Colin said.

"That's for sure."

This topic exhausted, neither of them said anything for a moment.

"So, how's your health?" he asked.

"My health?"

"I figure we've kind of done the weather."

"Yeah." She hopped over Freud's leash as, investigating a paper bag, he crossed abruptly in front of her. "Come on, heel." She gave an ineffectual pull.

"Well trained," Colin observed.

"Thank you." Trish pulled with both hands as Freud buried his head in the bag. "Come on, good dog, heel."

Colin reached over and gave the leash a tug.

"Determined," he said.

"Very. Come on, Freud."

Curiosity satisfied, Freud abandoned the bag and scampered forward. Trish started to cross Arlington Street to the Public Gardens, then paused to check for cars.

"Oh, kid, you're learning," he said.

"I'm not a kid."

"Right," he nodded. "Woman, you're learning."

She smiled at him and they crossed the street.

CHAPTER SIX

They strolled down the sodden cement path leading around toward the Beacon Street side of the park.

"Sure is wet," he said.

"Yeah," she agreed.

They kept walking. The park was quiet. Gray mist rose up from the pond, the ever-widening circles from falling raindrops bouncing off each other. There were a few ducks swimming, most of them gathered under the flimsy protection of the willow trees overhanging the edge of the water.

"Sure is different without the swanboats," she said.

"Yeah," he agreed. "Sure is."

Freud dragged over to the edge of the pond, barking at the ducks, some of whom flew off with great indignant splashes, most of whom ignored him.

"You know," Colin kept his hands deep in his pockets, "the mist's kind of beautiful."

"It is."

He stared up at the trees, branches framing the elegant Ritz Hotel and, rising tall behind it, the John Hancock Building.

"Never seems real," he said. "It's too nice." He shook his head. "I'd hate the country."

Trish laughed.

"What's so funny?" He glanced down, embarrassed.

"I'd hate living in the country too. Think there's something wrong with us?"

"Nothing some nice exhaust fumes won't cure." He shifted his position. "You, uh, you feel like sitting down for a minute?"

"Sure."

They ended up on a bench beneath a willow tree, close to the bridge over the pond.

"You know, you're crazy," she said. "You should zip that up."

"Can't get much wetter," he shrugged, looking down at his jacket which hung open. He picked up a stick. "Hey, dog, you fetch?"

"Sometimes." Trish took off his leash.

Colin threw it and Freud loped away, nosing the stick when it landed, then returning without it.

"He only fetches mahogany or oak," Trish explained.

"Yeah, right."

They sat without speaking for a long, wet minute.

"Do your parents know about me?" he asked.

"What do you mean?"

"You know." He wouldn't look at her. "That I'm stupid. That I've had detention for the last three years. That all your friends hate me."

"They don't—"

"Yeah, right. You tell them you were going out with me?"

"Well . . ." She hesitated.

"Scared to, huh?"

"No, I—"

"I should have figured." He kicked at the grass with his left foot.

"Well, I—I mean, I—"

"Don't waste your breath." He kicked harder at the clump of grass. "Why'd you even go out with me?"

"Because I wanted to get to know you."

"Lucky you."

"Well, I did," she said, defensive.

"Oh, great." He stood up. "Past tense."

"You know that's not what I meant."

"Yeah, sure." He shoved his hands into his pockets. "How come all your parents kept asking last night was

53

where I wanted to go to college? I'm probably not even going to graduate from high school!"

Trish didn't say anything.

"Yeah, that's what I figured." He shook his head. "I knew I shouldn't have asked you out, I knew it was a mistake."

"Then why did you?" she asked.

"I don't know. Because I'm stupid, I guess." He kicked the bench hard.

"Colin," she said, moving over to touch his arm.

"Leave me alone!" He shook her hand off. "I don't need pity, okay?"

"I wasn't—"

"Yeah, sure." He jammed his hands into his pockets, not looking at her. "I gotta go," he muttered.

"We just got here."

"Yeah, well, I gotta go." He started toward the bridge.

"Colin—"

He broke into a run, sneakers pounding against the wet cement as he ran up the steps to the bridge.

"Colin, wait!" she shouted after him.

He ran faster, across the bridge, toward the exit of the park.

"Hey." Colin's father grinned at him as he came into the kitchen twenty minutes later. His father was eating an early dinner, bent over the table in his police uniform. He was more muscular, but not much bigger than his son, with the same crisp, cowlick-ridden hair. "Still raining, is it?"

"Yeah," Colin said briefly, hanging his jacket over a chair to dry. He crossed to the cupboard, taking down a glass, then moving to the refrigerator to get a beer.

His father shook his head. "I could be arresting you for that, lad. What would Captain O'Reilly be thinking if he saw this?"

"That I was rotten." Colin tilted the glass and poured in half the bottle.

Mr. McNamara smiled. "He wouldn't be thinking that."

"You want one too?"

"I'm about to go on duty, and you're asking me if I want a beer?" Mr. McNamara shook his head again. Then he frowned. "Are you okay, Colin?"

Colin shrugged, sitting down.

"Were you out with that girl again?"

"Yeah."

"Did you have a nice time?"

Colin played with the salt shaker in the middle of the table.

"Teddy and Brian stopped over," his father said after a pause. "They were wanting to know if you'd go out tonight."

"Guess so." Colin refilled his glass. "I don't know, I got kind of a headache."

His father nodded. "Your mother's worried about you," he said.

"Yeah? Why?"

"She said you were upset last night, something about this girl."

"It's nothing to do with this girl."

"Nothing she said or anything?"

"It just didn't work out, okay?" Colin tore a piece of bread from the crusty loaf on the counter. "I shouldn't even have asked her out; I was stupid." He reached out to get a knife, winced, and used his right arm.

"Your shoulder bothering you again?"

"Always does when it rains." He spread some butter on the chunk of bread.

"Maybe you should be staying in tonight, putting some heat on it."

"I'm fine." Colin sat back down. "If your shift starts at four, you're going to be late."

"You're right, I am." Mr. McNamara drained his coffee mug, then picked up his badge and pinned it on.

"Arrest lots of delinquents."

"I hope not, I hate to arrest people." Mr. McNamara rinsed off his plate. "I'll never understand why they all can't . . . Colin?"

"What."

"I hate to see you so unhappy. Will you not worry, lad? So I don't have to worry?"

"You don't have to worry."

"I can't help it." Mr. McNamara unlocked a drawer in the buffet in the corner, took out his gun, loaded it, and dropped it slowly into his holster. Then he put on his cap, which fell to its usual tilt. "Don't be worrying about this girl, okay? There's lots of others, you'll meet a nice one."

"I did meet a nice one."

"Well, you'll meet others." He rested his hand on his son's shoulder. "Promise you'll put some heat on this, okay?"

Colin nodded.

"Good." Mr. McNamara started out of the room, then paused. "Colin, promise me you won't ever think I'm not proud of you, okay?"

"You've never been proud of me," Colin said.

"That's not true. If I get mad at you, it's only because—"

"You're late for work, Dad." Colin picked up Ophelia from the floor next to his chair, carried her past his father and down the hall to his bedroom.

CHAPTER SEVEN

That night, Trish, Janet, and Rachael were slouched in easy chairs in Rachael's family room, watching a television movie.

"The blond kid's kind of quiet," Rachael commented to Janet.

"Maybe she's too busy eating," Janet said, shrugging as she took a chocolate-chip cookie from the package on the table.

"Maybe she's just embarrassed because we spent so much time talking about your date and didn't even ask her about hers."

Trish looked away from the television.

"My date?" she asked.

"Kind of sad when someone who's supposed to be a good friend calls up and hears about it from someone's little brother," Rachael said.

"It's really sad," Janet agreed.

Trish flushed, and took three chocolate-chip cookies. "I guess maybe I should have mentioned it."

"Might have been nice," Rachael said.

"I don't know." Trish drank some Tab. "I thought you guys might make fun of me, or try and talk me out of it. Or he'd get scared and chicken out. I wanted to see if it would work out."

"Did it?" Janet asked.

Trish looked at the couple in the movie: they were passionately embracing.

"No," she said in a low voice.

Rachael shrugged. "So forget him. Fall in love with someone decent."

Trish scowled. "Why don't you get off me?" she asked. "He's a nice guy."

Rachael looked at her, eyes expressionless behind her glasses. "Sorry," she said.

"Janet went parking," Trish went on. "Why don't you get on her?"

"Leave me out of it," Janet said, watching the movie.

"Yeah, well, it's true," Trish said grumpily.

"It's not like Peter's a sex maniac," Rachael pointed out.

"Colin isn't either."

"What about Diane Harris?"

Trish took another cookie, breaking it into three pieces. "What about her?"

"He's a sex maniac," Janet said.

"I thought you wanted to be left out of this." Trish slouched down. "All he did was kiss me goodnight."

Rachael grinned impishly. "Tongue or not?" she asked.

Trish scowled again, getting up and heading for the door.

"Where are you going?" Rachael also stood up. "Trish, come on."

"Come on where?" Trish asked. "You won't even give him a chance. You're supposed to be my friend, remember?"

"I *am* being your friend."

"Hey, cut it out, you guys." Janet gave up on trying to watch the movie. "It's not worth arguing about."

"I think it is," Trish said.

Rachael sighed. "I think he's a jerk, okay? Look at the way he gets in fights all the time. How do you know he wouldn't turn around and slug you someday?"

"We're in a fight," Trish said. "How do I know *you* won't turn around and slug me?"

Rachael laughed, sitting back down. "Touché," she said.

Trish returned to her easy chair. "He *is* nice."

"How many guys have you gone out with?"

"I don't know. Not that many," she admitted.

"Not that many," Rachael agreed. "Look, if we went skiing and I said I wanted to go down an expert trail, would you let me?"

"Sure. If you wanted to enough."

"You would not," Rachael scoffed. "I've never been on skis in my life."

"Yeah, but if you wanted to—"

"You'd at least let me know what I was getting into."

Trish slouched over her Tab, aware that she had lost that one. "Maybe," she said.

"I just don't want to see you get in trouble, okay?"

"It doesn't matter. I'm not going to see him again anyway."

"Yeah, but you know what it's going to be like at school when everyone hears about it. You know what people think about anyone who'd go out with him. Guys especially'll say stuff."

"I know," Trish sighed. "That's why I was scared to tell anyone."

"I would have been too. Colin McNamara." Rachael shuddered. She reached forward to get a cookie. "Speaking of guys, Mike Pilsner kept following me around last night and asking where you were."

"Speaking of sex maniacs," Trish said.

"Yeah, really," Rachael agreed. "I like guys who are built, but he's—I bet he'll be *really* obnoxious when he finds out you went out with McNamara."

"I don't understand him." Trish opened her second Tab. "I almost never even talk to him. How come he's such a pain?"

"He's a football player," Janet said. "Those guys think we all just fall down lusting over them."

Rachael shrugged. "Some of them aren't bad." She grinned at Trish. "If you were going to fall for a hood, you could have at least found one with a decent body."

"No comment," Trish said.

* * *

It was Sunday morning, and Mrs. Masters decided that she wanted to go on a fall foliage drive.

"Come on, Ben, it's beautiful out." She put her hands on her husband's shoulders as he sat at the table, eating brunch.

"Waste of gas," he grumbled, reading the *Times Book Review*.

"The leaves come once a year, it's worth it. We'll stop somewhere, get some apples, find an old bookstore, take Freud's picture in front of something rustic." She moved her hands around his neck. "Sounds like fun, right?"

"I'd rather stay home and read the *Times*."

"Greg, don't you think it'd be swell?" She moved down the table, putting her arm around her son.

"I was gonna play football with the guys." Greg poured more maple syrup on his pancakes.

"Football players are gross," Trish said, not looking up from her book.

"Yeah, so are ugly sisters—hey, ow!" He grabbed his shin. "Mom, she kicked me!"

"Don't antagonize him," Mrs. Masters said. "And put that book down, I hate it when you read at the table."

"*The Old Man and the Sea?*" Greg asked. "That sounds pretty stupid."

"Greg, if you come with us," Mrs. Masters said, changing the subject, "we'll stop and get ice cream."

"Wow, really?" he asked. "I'm coming!"

"Good, then it's decided." Mrs. Masters got herself some more orange juice and sat down.

"It is?" Mr. Masters looked up from the *Times*.

"It is. And stop reading at the table." She frowned. "Trish, why aren't you eating? Are you sick?"

"Pancakes make you fat," Trish said.

"Don't look now," Mrs. Masters said to the other two, "but I think we've been insulted."

Trish shook her head. "You're not fat. I told you I didn't want any, Mom. I'm on a diet."

Mrs. Masters leaned over the table to look at her daughter.

"Why?" She sat back.

"Because I ate about six hundred cookies last night."

"It shows too," Mrs. Masters agreed. "Look at her, isn't she disgusting? You are coming to look at leaves with us, right?"

"We're going to look at leaves?" Trish put her book down.

Her mother nodded.

"But we went last week."

Her mother nodded.

"Oh, wow." Trish bit her lip. "Will you hate me if I sort of pass? I have a trig test tomorrow, and I don't know anything."

"Junior year's the most important," Mr. Masters said; Trish nodded.

"Besides," Trish grinned at her mother, "you know we're going to end up going for a foliage drive next week too."

"The leaves only come once a year," Mrs. Masters said.

"I know. So can I pass till next week?"

"If you have some breakfast."

"Deal." Trish helped herself to two pancakes.

"Diet willpower," Mr. Masters remarked.

When her parents and Greg were gone, Trish wandered around the town house for a while, restless. She patted Freud for a few minutes, then went to find Dumpling and pat him too. She gave each animal some chicken from dinner the night before, then sat down at the kitchen table, staring at the phone. Finally, she took a deep breath and picked up the phone book, flipping to the M's.

"Oh, wow." She stared at the list of McNamaras, easily a hundred names. She didn't know his father's first name. She sighed and closed the book. Then she reopened it, finding the page and putting her finger on an arbitrary name. "Yeah, Theodore." She shrugged. "Maybe his name's

Theodore." She tried the name aloud. "Ted McNamara. Yeah, that sounds good." She picked up the phone and dialed. The phone rang twice; a woman answered. "Hi, may I please speak to Colin? . . . Oh. I'm sorry, I must have the wrong number." She hung up the phone. "This is stupid." She studied the book again. "Donald. Hmmm. Maybe his name's Donald." She dialed the number. "Hello, may I please speak to Colin? . . . Oh. Sorry." She put the phone down.

Giving up, she took a Tab from the refrigerator, picked up *The Old Man and the Sea* from the counter, and brought it out to the living room to read. She was only on the third chapter when the doorbell rang.

It was probably one of Greg's friends, she decided, wanting to know if Greg could come out and play football. But when she opened the door, she saw Colin standing there instead.

"Uh, hi," he said.

"Hi." She stepped back, uneasy.

"Can I come in?" He shifted his weight from one foot to the other, hands in his pockets.

"Oh, yeah," Trish said, snapping out of it. "Yeah, right." She opened the door all the way, dropping the book on the table behind her so he wouldn't see it.

"Did I, uh, come at a bad time?" he asked.

She shook her head. "I wasn't doing anything. My parents and Greg went out."

"Oh." He looked worried. "You like, not allowed to have people here when they're not home?"

"No, it's okay. Come on, I was in here."

He followed her into the living room, but didn't sit down.

"I came over to apologize," he said. "I'm sorry I was such a jerk yesterday."

"You weren't—"

"Don't bother, okay?" He sat on the couch, but not really near her. "Were you, like, embarrassed to tell your parents about me?"

"I don't *know* about you," she said.

"No, guess you don't." He concentrated on a small rip at the knee of his right jeans leg. "I don't know. I—" he swallowed—"I'm not so great at talking to people. I kind of don't do it much, you know?"

She nodded, moving a little closer. He didn't react and she picked up his hand, holding it in both of hers.

"How come you're so nice to me?" he asked. "I'm such a jerk to you."

"I don't think you're a jerk."

"You don't know me too well," he said.

She didn't say anything, but caressed his hand; he let her do it, not speaking either.

"I got hit by a car when I was a little kid," he said suddenly.

She nodded, waiting for him to go on.

"I was seven. Kind of crossed the street right into a car. It's why I'm so careful now." He shifted his position, ending up closer. "I missed, like, a year of school."

"What did you hurt?"

"My shoulder and back, mostly. Got a concussion and everything too."

"I'm sorry," she said.

"The whole thing kind of screwed me up. Especially with school."

"Because you missed so much?"

"That, too. Think they figured I was hurt so long I got brain damage." He tried to smile. "I *was* doing some stuttering." He withdrew his hand from hers, slouched down with his arms across his chest. "My IQ's, like, borderline."

"Because you get scared on tests?"

He glanced at her. "You don't think it's because I'm stupid?"

"I know you're not stupid."

"Everyone at school thinks I am."

"Everyone at school is wrong."

He moved closer, and she lifted her arm up around his shoulders.

"They put me in all remedial classes," he said. "I couldn't even hack that."

"Did you try?"

"I was scared to. I didn't want to be stupid." He ran a quick, embarrassed hand through his hair. "My father used to show me these flashcards every night. I could never do them. I was scared I might get one wrong and he'd get mad at me."

"Would he have?"

"I doubt it. I was scared he would, though. Most of my teachers got mad." He half-smiled, but his mouth was shaking. "Guess I was a real mental case."

Trish put her other arm around him and kissed his cheek.

"What was that for?" he asked uneasily.

"I thought you needed it."

"Don't be nice just because you feel sorry for me." He kept himself stiff.

She hugged him again.

"I wasn't stupid." His voice shook. "I really wasn't."

"I know."

"I used to read all the time. I just didn't tell anyone."

"Do your parents know?"

"Not for the first couple of years, but yeah. They got me all kinds of tutors, but I never—" He shook his head. "I guess now they think I'm going to pull myself together. My father used to get pretty mad. Like, I got caught shoplifting a couple of times, and he threw a fit. He was always after me to shape up." He sighed. "I don't know. I guess they decided to stop trying."

"Maybe they just decided not to push you anymore."

"Maybe they just decided I was stupid."

"You know," Trish slid her hand up his neck and into the dark, wavy hair, "to look at you at school, I'd figure you were about the most confident person around."

"To look at me, you'd probably figure I should be in reform school."

"No, I wouldn't."

"Guess you didn't figure I'm some dumb guy who's afraid to even cross the street by himself."

"I still don't."

He stood up, hands going into his pockets, and turned to face her.

"What's wrong with you?" he demanded.

"What do you mean?"

"I mean, there's got to be something wrong with you."

"Oh." She thought for a second. "Well, I broke my leg when I was twelve. . . ."

"I meant, is there anything wrong with you as a person."

She stared at him. "Are you kidding?"

"I swear you seem like you're perfect. I was scared to death to even walk by you."

"But—" She blushed. "I mean, there are thousands of things wrong with me."

"Like what?"

"Like, I can be really bitchy, and—and I pick on Greg, and I come home and sulk and make everyone else in a bad mood, and—"

He sat down next to her, grinning. "Isn't there anything good about you?" He put his arm around her.

"Sorry."

"Well, I'd better give you a hug." He held her for a minute. "God, you're the first girl I—well, it's been a while."

Trish stiffened involuntarily.

"Oh, that." He let go, the brooding, distant expression back. "You're hung up about *that,* aren't you?"

"About what?" Trish didn't meet his eyes.

"You know what else is wrong with you? You're a rotten liar." He stood up. "Damn it!"

"It doesn't bother me," Trish said, trying to sound convincing. "Really."

"Yeah, sure it doesn't." He paced nervously across the room.

"Look, Colin, it really doesn't bother me. I mean . . ."

"If I tell you something," he said, meeting her eyes strongly, "will you promise not to tell anyone else? I mean, anyone? Ever?"

She nodded.

"I'm not kidding, Trish."

"I won't tell anyone."

He held her gaze until he was sure, then nodded.

"Okay." He leaned against one of the sets of bookshelves. "I *was* sleeping with Diane; no use saying I wasn't. Is that the part that bothers you?"

"You know it isn't."

"Yeah." He sighed. "I'm not stupid, Trish. I know about protection. We went out for about three months. I would have broken it off sooner, but I got hung up with the whole sex thing." He focused on the shelf holding Trish's tennis trophy. "Anyway, the last time we were going to do it, she had her period, so we didn't. We broke up right after that. And then she shows up pregnant."

"It wasn't you," Trish said.

"No. Like I said, I know about protection."

"But you took the blame."

"What else could I do?" He hunched his shoulders. "She never saw the guy again, she couldn't pay for it—I couldn't just let her—well, I had to. Someone had to."

"But you let everyone think—"

"Not my parents," he said quickly. "I'd never do that to them. I didn't figure anyone else mattered."

"But how could you—"

"What's it matter?" He kicked at the carpet with one foot. "Whole stupid school hates me."

"Not the *whole* school."

He looked up. "Yeah?"

She nodded, leaning forward to kiss him.

CHAPTER EIGHT

They broke apart hastily, hearing the front door open.

"Trish?" Mrs. Masters called.

"Yeah, in here." Trish jumped into a rocking chair, halfway across the room from Colin.

Her mother followed her voice and came in, obviously surprised to see Colin.

"Hi, Mrs. Masters," he said, very flustered, jumping to his feet.

"Hi," she smiled. "Please, sit down."

"Y-you had a good drive?" Trish asked.

"Very nice."

"Nancy?" Mr. Masters shouted from the front door. "Help!"

"I told you not to carry those things by yourself." She left the room to help him.

"I ought to get going," Colin said.

"Are you sure?"

"Yeah." He fumbled for his sweater, pulling it on. Trish followed him to the front door.

"You have fun, Dad?" she asked.

"In spite of myself. Hi, Colin. Have an apple." He handed Colin the apple Mrs. Masters had left him and headed for the kitchen.

Colin looked at the apple. "You want this?"

"It's yours."

He shrugged and polished it on the front of his sweater.

"Walk me to the sidewalk?" he asked.

Outside, they stood awkwardly by the curb.

"Yeah," Colin said.

"Yeah what?"

"You're not mad at me anymore, right?"

She touched his arm. "I'm not mad."

"Good."

"I'm glad you came over."

"Really?" He checked her expression.

"No, I just said it to make you feel better." She slid her hand down to his. "Of course I'm glad, what do you think?"

"I don't very often." He looked at her front door. "Can I kiss you, or will they see?"

"I don't know," she followed his gaze. "They might."

"I'll risk it." He leaned forward and kissed her, hanging on for a second.

"Hi!" Greg said cheerfully, running past them with his football, heading for Boston Common. "Wait till I tell Mom, Trish!"

The two broke apart, and Greg took off before Trish could grab him.

"I'm sorry," Trish said and he shrugged. "I am glad you came over."

"Me too." He moved back a couple of steps, hands going into his pockets. "I'll, uh, I'll see you in school tomorrow?"

"Okay."

"Okay." He nodded. "Well, see you."

"Okay," she said.

"Guess I'll be in my room if anyone wants me," Colin said after dinner.

"Lots of homework?" his mother asked.

Colin shrugged.

His father flipped on the television. "Will you be getting your report card soon?"

"I guess."

"And are you doing okay?"

Colin looked at him.

"What do you think, Dad?" he asked. "Look, I'll be in

my room." He found Ophelia in the hall and carried her with him. "Good day, kid?" He smiled at the small, whiskered face. Ophelia purred, rubbing her head against his chin. "Yeah, me too," he said. "Well, kind of." He opened the door to his room, balancing Ophelia against his shoulder. "You know something?" He sat on his bed, still holding her. "She's almost as easy as you to talk to."

Ophelia purred.

"I'm not kidding." He hugged his cat closer. "Like, she's really something. If I had a yearbook, I'd show you her picture. She's beautiful. But I don't know, I gotta watch it." He leaned back against his pillows. "She'll wanna get out of it when people start hassling her, and I know they will. So I gotta be ready when she does that, right? I can't like her so much." He looked at Ophelia, who purred. With one last hug, he put her down on his pillow. "I'd better practice—you can watch."

He moved to his bookcase, studying the titles. After a moment's thought, he pulled out *Long Day's Journey into Night*. He sat down on his desk and leafed through it with a practiced hand. He stopped at one page, bending it back, crossing abstractedly to his bed to lean against the footboard, back to the door. Then he stared forward at nothing, looking at an imaginary character, his expression suddenly tired, slightly drunken. Lowering the book, he started speaking, his voice deep, resigned, bitter.

" 'It was a great mistake, my being born a man,' " he said. " 'I would have been much more successful as a seagull, or a fish. As it is, I will always be a stranger who never feels at home, who does not really want and is not really wanted, who can never belong, who must always be a little in love with death.' "

Hearing a gasp, he turned to see his father at the door.

"Good God." Mr. McNamara didn't come in. "Are you practicing, lad, or do you really feel that way?"

Colin laughed, putting the book down.

"I'm just practicing," he said. "Some speech, huh?"

"You do it too well." Mr. McNamara came in and leaned back against his son's desk. "You're getting good, lad. You'll have trouble convincing me you don't really feel that way."

"I don't." Colin laughed again. "It's just a good one to read."

"Well, do another."

"Huh?" Colin blushed. "Dad, I was only playing around, I—"

"So, read me another," his father said, shrugging. "Something more cheerful."

"From this play?"

"Just read something." Mr. McNamara folded his arms across his chest. "I'd like to hear it."

"Dad . . ."

"You're wanting to be an actor and you're shy in front of your own father? Just read a little part."

Colin flipped slowly through the book.

"Uh, how about the part where the father's talking about acting?" he asked.

"Great, I love that." Mr. McNamara nodded. "Want me to be Edmund? I can just sit here, and you can look at me."

"Okay." Colin grinned. "We're, like, both kind of drunk and we're playing cards."

"What're we playing?"

Colin grinned harder. "Go fish."

"Are you sure?" His father frowned. "I don't seem to be remembering that."

"We're playing casino." Colin took a deck of cards out of his desk and dealt his father some, taking a few for himself. He dragged a chair over and settled down across from him. He glanced at the script, shifted his position, and glanced up, his expression changing again: sad, intense, a little proud. " 'I was considered one of the three or four young actors with the greatest promise in America. I'd worked like hell. I'd left a good job as a machinist to take supers' parts because I loved the theatre. I was wild with ambition. I read all the plays ever written. I studied Shakespeare as you'd study the Bible. I educated myself. I got rid of an Irish brogue you could cut with a knife.' " Colin paused, more and more into the part. " 'I loved Shakespeare. I would have acted in any of his plays for nothing, for the joy of being alive in his great poetry. And I acted well in him. I felt inspired by him. I could have been a great Shakespearean actor if I'd kept on, I know that!' " He stopped, suddenly embarrassed, putting down his cards. "God, I'm getting worked up in that, huh?"

"You're good," his father said quietly. "Very good. You were getting me worked up in it too."

Colin shrugged, still embarrassed, putting the book back on the shelf.

"I wish you'd try out for a play at school." Mr. McNamara realized that he still had his cards and put them down. "It'd do you good to get involved over there. You'd meet some nice people, and you might feel better about school."

"Who says I don't feel good about school?"

"I said it would make you feel *better*, lad."

"What, are you mad now?"

"Did I say I was?"

"Yeah, well." Colin shifted his weight. "The drama club's really queer. Besides, they give all the good parts to the same guy; they wouldn't want me."

"I can't believe there's anyone over there who's better than you. You're good, lad. You should let them know it."

"They wouldn't want me," Colin insisted.

"How do you know till you try?"

"I know, okay? I'm not stupid!"

"I know you're not." Mr. McNamara got up, his hands going into his pockets, looking very much like his son. "But you need school. Your mother and I have always wanted you to go to college and you can't if you don't try."

"Who says I want to go?" Colin concentrated on his bookshelf. "You're the one that wants me to go."

"I want you to be happy. And you won't be if—"

"How do you know?" Colin's temper went completely. "You always do this! Face it, I'm stupid! I probably won't even graduate! What's it matter?"

"It matters a lot," his father said quietly.

"Yeah, well—" Colin stopped, trying to get control. "Just leave me alone, Dad. Can't we get off it?"

"If you want." Face stiff, his father headed for the door.

"So now you'll go get mad at Mom and it'll be my fault?"

His father looked back at him, expressionless.

"I wouldn't be taking this out on your mother," he said. "She worries enough as it is."

"And what, is that my fault?"

"Sometimes."

"Yeah, well, sorry." Colin kept his back to his father. "Maybe I would have done better as a stupid seagull."

"You probably feel that way."

Colin heard the door shut and listened to him move down the hall. He waited a few more guilty seconds, then went out after him.

"Dad?"

"What?" His father paused without turning.

"I'm sorry. I didn't mean to hurt your feelings."

"Who says you did?" His father still didn't turn around.

"Well, I didn't mean to."

His father nodded, continuing down the hall.

"Dad?"

He paused again. "What?"

"I don't want to be a seagull either."

CHAPTER NINE

Trish was restless in homeroom Monday morning, jumping every time the door opened.

"What's with you?" Rachael asked, reading her French.

"Nothing."

"He probably won't even show up."

The door opened and Colin came in, not quite slouching, not quite sauntering. His shirt was tucked in, and he had evidently spent some time trying to get his hair under control.

"You're late, McNamara," Mr. Bradford growled from the front of the room.

"Sorry." Colin flashed the grin.

"You have a pass?"

"Yeah."

Mr. Bradford's eyes came up from the attendance book. "You do?"

Colin moved to the front of the room, dropping the limp piece of paper on the book, then turning to find a seat.

"Teacher's pet!" a boy laughed as he passed.

Colin kept going, grinning and cuffing the boy on the side of the head. As he got near Trish, he hesitated, looking at her, then at his friends, not sure where to sit. He thrust his hands defensively into his pockets.

"How about sitting down, McNamara?" Mr. Bradford grumbled.

"Uh, yeah." Colin swallowed, seemingly poised to run. He sucked in a deep breath and sat in the desk on Trish's other side, as all the boys in the back whistled.

"Go for it, Mac!" one yelled.

"Watch out, she uses big words!" another laughed.

Most of the girls in the room stared at Trish with sympathetic Thank-God-he-didn't-decide-to-sit-next-to-me looks. A stocky blond boy in a rumpled T-shirt came up the other side of her desk.

"Whatcha do?" he leered. "Write your name on a bathroom wall somewhere?"

"Get off her, Mitch." Colin's voice was low.

"What is she," the boy laughed. "Your *biology* tutor?"

"Anatomy, more likely," someone said, and all the boys laughed.

Colin scowled, but made himself relax, putting his feet on his desk.

"She's a beautiful woman," he said. "Sometimes I like to sit next to beautiful women."

Watching the scene, Mr. Bradford spoke up.

"Why don't you leave her alone, McNamara?" he suggested. "Stop bothering her."

"He's not," Trish said quickly and everyone laughed.

"Oooh," a boy grinned. "Take it off!"

Trish and Colin looked in opposite directions, embarrassed.

When the bell rang, a boy from the back sauntered up with a matchbook, which he dropped on Trish's desk with a theatrical flourish.

"My phone number," he announced. "Anytime, chick." He grinned at her. "She doesn't dress like your type, Mac."

"Nicky, your nose looks better on your face; you know what I mean?" Colin stood up, his right fist clenching.

"Wow, you must be pretty good, chick." Nicky gave Trish a big wink and headed for the door, still grinning.

"See you in French, Trish." Rachael gathered up her books.

"Yeah." Trish was getting hers together more slowly.

The room cleared fast, as people hurried off to get the new rumors flying.

"Well, now what?" Colin asked pugnaciously. "Am I supposed to walk you to class or something?"

Hurt by the irritation in his voice, Trish pushed past him to the door.

"I didn't know there were rules," she said coolly.

"Hey, look." He caught up to her as she stepped out into the hall. "I'm sorry, I didn't mean it that way." He noticed the people passing—all staring, some grinning, some frowning. "Oh, no."

"Yeah, really," Trish agreed, also seeing the looks.

"Uh, look," he ran one hand through his hair. "Will you, like, be upset if I kind of don't walk you to class?"

"No."

"You sure?"

"Hey, Mac!" a boy shouted. "With that kind of scoring, you should have tried out for football!"

Most of the people who heard laughed.

"I'm very sure," Trish said.

"Good." He hesitated, then leaned toward her.

"What are you doing?" She moved back a step, instinctively clutching her books.

"Uh, well . . ." His hand went back through his hair. "I was sort of going to kiss you."

Trish stayed back. "Why?"

"Why? What do you mean, why? That's what you do."

She shook her head. "Uh-uh."

"What do you mean? If the guy doesn't walk the girl to class, he just kisses her before."

"Well, I don't."

"You don't?" he asked uneasily.

She shook her head.

"Oh." He took a few steps backward. "Uh, why not?"

"In public?"

"No one's looking." He glanced. "Well okay, everyone's looking."

"Yeah," she nodded. "Um, I'm going to be late to class."

"Yeah. Well, you'd better go, then." He shoved his

hands into his pockets. "Especially before anyone else sees you with me."

"Colin—"

"Later." He pushed his way down the hall, not looking back.

"Yeah," Trish said. "Later." As she started down the hall, a hulking boy she didn't even know fell into step with her.

"You guys break up already?" he asked, eyes moving up and down. "I'm free."

Trish hugged her books to her chest. "I'm not."

"I'm willing to pay," he smirked.

Trish's eyes widened and she stopped abruptly.

"Hey, Trish," Rachael called, appearing from nowhere. "Excuse me," she said to the boy, and steered Trish up the hall. "Come on, we're going to be late."

Trish gulped. "I thought you went to French."

"I thought you might run into trouble." Rachael glanced behind them.

"I didn't know it was going to be this bad."

"How'd you think it was going to be? I bet Janet's getting harassed all over the place, and Peter's a decent guy." She noticed her friend's expression. "I'm sorry. You know what I mean."

"Hey, look," Trish said stiffly. "Don't feel you have to be on my side in this."

"I'm going to be on your side whether I go along with the thing or not."

"What's the point?"

"We're friends, right? Besides, you're not stupid. If you think he's okay, I don't know, maybe he is."

"He is," Trish said.

"If you say so." Then Rachael grinned. "Cheer up, it could be worse."

"How?"

"He could be black." Rachael laughed and opened the door to the French room.

* * *

It was later, and Colin strolled down the hall, avoiding his remedial-reading class. A boy in a faded green T-shirt caught up with him.

"Hey, Mac."

"Hey, Teddy," he nodded. "Skipping class?"

"What the hell. What you got, reading?"

"Yeah."

"You ever gonna break down and let them teach you how?"

Colin looked at him.

"I don't know," he said. "Maybe sometime."

Teddy nodded, then grinned at him.

"Trish Masters, huh?"

Colin blushed. "Sort of."

"Not bad." Teddy punched him on the arm. "Good-looking chick."

Colin blushed more.

"Never would've thought it, Mac."

"Why not?"

"Hell, I don't know." Teddy pulled out a cigarette as they got to the stairwell, and sat down, offering the pack. "You smoking this week?"

"No," Colin laughed, sitting two steps lower.

"Gotta keep the old voice in shape, huh?" Teddy let out a cloud of smoke. "Or you just worried about your breath?"

"Both, I guess."

"Yeah, I bet." Teddy inhaled. "Never would've thought it."

"Like I said, how come?"

"Hell, I had her pegged as a virgin."

Colin straightened up, the smile leaving his face.

"She is," he said quietly. "At least, as far as I know."

"Not for long."

"Hey," Colin grabbed his arm. "Don't be saying stuff like that!"

"Whatsa matter, Mac?" Teddy pulled free. "How far you gotten?"

Furious, Colin jerked him up, drawing back his fist.

"You keep your mouth shut about her," he growled. "It's not like that, and it's not going to be!"

"Sorry, Father McNamara." Teddy shoved him away. "Forget I—"

"Hey, what's going on down there?" A teacher came striding down the hall. "Jackson, put it out!"

Teddy snorted, slowly stubbing his cigarette out on the banister.

"I gotta go," he said. "I'm late to class." He started up the stairs. "Don't forget, Mac. I want seconds."

Colin started to go after him, but the teacher yanked him back.

"Don't get yourself in more trouble," the teacher advised. "Where you supposed to be?"

"Reading," Colin muttered, scowling up the stairs, fists tight.

"Well, do you really think you can afford to miss that, McNamara?" the teacher asked. "Maybe you ought to get moving."

"Yeah, anything you say." Colin shook the man's hand off, heading down the hall.

"Hey, McNamara!" the teacher called after him.

"What."

"Watch your step."

Colin slouched lower and kept going. He pushed on the door of the Reading Room and noisily entered. His teacher, Miss Nelson, looked up from the table where she was sitting with five other students. She was young and earnest, with constantly slipping tortoise-shell glasses.

"You're late, Colin." She pushed her glasses up.

"Yeah, and I don't have a pass, neither." He sat down, feet swinging up onto the low table.

"Where's your book?"

"Dunno. Somewheres at home, I guess." Colin yawned,

untucking his shirt. "Hey, go on with the class. Don't let me interrupt."

Miss Nelson crossed the room to a set of crowded bookshelves, and pulled out a copy of the book. She returned to the table, and handed it to him.

"We're on page fifteen," she said.

"Can't count that high." He handed back the book.

She opened it to the right page and returned it to him.

"Why don't you read aloud?" she suggested. "From the top of the page."

Colin looked at the words for a minute, then put the book down.

"It's too hard," he said.

"Why don't you try? We'll help you."

"I don't need help from anyone." He gave his book to the boy sitting next to him. "Mario, read it already." He smiled as everyone but Miss Nelson laughed. "See, like, when I'm a real important executive, I'll have my secretaries read for me. I can have 'em stay after work and like, teach me things."

"Heard you just hired a new secretary," one of the boys further down the table commented.

"Yeah, what of it?" Colin's hands moved into fists.

"What you gonna teach *her?*"

Colin got up from his seat. "Robby, you say one more thing and I'm gonna break your stupid face in half."

"Colin, sit down." Miss Nelson got in front of him. "Now."

Colin looked at her, then slowly lowered himself down, fists tight.

"Good." Miss Nelson returned to her seat, pulling a stack of dittoed sheets out of a manila folder. "Why don't you all close your books and we'll spend the rest of the period on these."

"What is it?" Colin asked as she handed him two dittos. "Some kind of test?"

"Only a diagnostic one."

Colin frowned, pushing the sheets away.

"Remember, these are just to find out what you know," Miss Nelson said, passing out the rest of the papers. "So don't worry if there are words you don't know. Just do your best." She sat down, then noticed Colin slouched in his chair with his arms across his chest. "Colin?"

"I don't have a pencil," he said.

She took one out of her purse, handing it down to him. "You can have it," she said. "I have plenty of others."

He shrugged, not picking it up.

"Why don't you start?" she suggested. "We only have about fifteen more minutes before the bell rings."

"I don't like pencil," he said. "It gets all over my hands."

She opened her purse, taking out two pens; one blue, one black.

"I don't like pens either."

"If he's not doing it, I'm not doing it," a girl at the end of the table said.

"Don't worry, Barbara," Miss Nelson said. "Just work on your own paper."

"But he always gets out of it."

"Just work on your own paper." Miss Nelson walked over to Colin's chair. "What would you rather write with?" she asked quietly.

"I dunno," he shrugged. "You got a green crayon?"

She nodded, crossing to the desk at the front of the room.

"Forget it," he said. "I don't want a stupid crayon."

"Colin, look," she said, coming back. "There's nothing to be nervous about. I only want to see how much of the last unit you learned."

"I didn't learn any of it."

"Oh, come on. I know you know at least some of these words." She ran her finger down the page. "Here." She paused at a multiple choice question. "Who did you say you were going to have read for you when you're a real important executive?"

"I dunno. I forget."

"Well, try to remember. Who is the person who would answer the phones and type all of your letters?"

"I dunno."

"Who answers the phones and types all the letters here at school?"

"I dunno," he said. "Mrs. Taylor."

"Right. And what's the word for her job?"

"How would I know?" he asked, scowling. "Ask her."

"Boy, is he stupid," Robby said.

Miss Nelson frowned at him. "That's enough out of you, Robby."

"Yeah, but this thing is so easy." Robby pointed to the test. "He must be retarded or something."

"First of all, you know that's not true," Miss Nelson said. "Second, if I hear one more word out of you, you'll be in here for detention today." She put her hand on Colin's shoulder. "Just try it, okay? No pressure."

Colin picked up the pencil, gripping it tightly, staring at the test. It *did* look kind of easy, but lots of times tests looked easy. Teachers always put in words like desert and dessert, affect and effect. If he got nervous and put down the wrong answer, they would think he was stupid. Like in the fourth grade. Once he forgot his coat before recess and when he came back to get it, he heard his teacher talking to another teacher, saying, "I don't know what to do about Colin McNamara's parents. They're convinced he's a genius. I think he's one of the slowest boys I've ever had." From then on, he was even more scared on tests. He knew teachers were watching him, waiting for him to make mistakes. Once he got everything right on a test and the teacher thought he was cheating. She made him come in after school and take a new test, sitting all by himself. The test was much harder and he couldn't even finish it, his hand cramping around his pencil, the words blurring. The teacher had frowned and taken the test away. Then she had called his parents and told them he had cheated. His parents had been furious at him. Now, even hearing the word "test" made him scared and during exams, he would always stare at his paper, afraid to look around in case the teacher thought he was cheating, afraid to put answers down in case they were all wrong.

The bell rang and he closed his eyes, letting the pencil drop out of his hand. Miss Nelson picked up all of the papers, coming over to him last. She looked at the test, seeing all of the blank answer spaces.

"Do you maybe want to come in after school and try again?" she asked.

"I'm busy after school," he said.

"Well then, how about now? I'm free this period."

"I have math."

"That's okay, I'll write you a pass."

He shook his head, standing up and slouching over to the door. Miss Nelson came after him.

"I know you can do it, Colin," she said. "Lots of people get nervous on tests. What if we try giving you an oral one?"

He scowled at her. "Why don't you face it? I'm stupid."

"But, you're not. I've watched your eyes when we're reading in class—they don't even hesitate. I don't think you're having trouble reading at all. I think you just—"

He pushed past her to the door. "I gotta go."

"Colin, come on. For once, can't you—"

"I gotta go!" he said and left the room, almost running.

CHAPTER TEN

Trish felt someone behind her as she got her lunch out of her locker and turned, hoping that it was Colin. Mike Pilsner towered above her, all teeth and muscles.

"Was looking for you Saturday night," he said.

"Oh?"

"Heard you had a good time."

"Oh."

"Yeah." He put his hand on her arm. "Wish I could have been there."

"Why, do you like movies?" Trish said, shaking the hand off.

"Depends on the rating." He lowered his voice. "You busy tonight?"

Trish just started for the cafeteria.

"Hey, come on." He pulled her back. "You're not gonna tell me you *like* that twerp, are you?"

"Mike, leave me alone."

"God, that kid can't even lift his hands over his head. You know how much I can press?"

Trish started for the cafeteria again.

"Two eighty, I can press." He caught up with her. "And I wasn't even trying."

"Well, that's good," she said politely.

"Damn right it is, more than almost anyone else on the team. How much you think that twerp could do?"

"I really don't know." Hurrying toward her usual table, Trish saw everyone good-naturedly teasing Janet and Peter, who were shyly sitting next to each other. As Trish sat down, the jokes stopped and everyone looked uneasy.

"If it isn't Typhoid Mary," Rachael said cheerfully.

"Funny." Trish opened her lunch bag.

"I kind've thought so." Rachael looked up and down the table. "Hey, come on, you guys, cut it out."

People began eating, quickly starting conversations.

"Hey, Trish." A girl leaned across the table. "You're not *really* seeing him, are you?"

"I don't know."

"But, he's so obnoxious."

"That's for sure," the girl next to her agreed. "How could you watch a movie with *him* next to you?"

"I don't go to watch the movie," Trish said.

"Wait a minute, wait a minute," Rachael broke in, her mouth full. She chewed quickly and swallowed. "The idea is to stop rumors, not make them worse."

"*You* don't like him, do you, Rachael?" one of the girls asked, her nose wrinkled in distaste.

"I can't stand him," Rachael admitted. "But I don't really know him."

"He's a nice—" Trish started. There was some sort of commotion toward the back of the noisy room, and she turned to see Colin going after a boy in a green T-shirt. His fists were doubled up, his expression furious.

"I wasn't kidding, Teddy!" he yelled. "You'd better take that back!"

"What, are you crazy, Mac?" Teddy retreated toward the wall.

"Hey, break it up!" A teacher monitoring the cafeteria ran over and grabbed Colin.

"But he—" Colin struggled to get away.

"Don't you ever quit, McNamara?" The teacher gave him an irritated shove. "Get down to the office and cool off. Jackson, take your seat."

Colin recovered his balance, then stared at the teacher, his fists clenching again.

"You'd better watch the pushing, mister," he said. "You can't be doing that to me."

"None of your mouth." The teacher shoved him forward. "I said, get down to the office, and I mean now!"

"And I said, watch the pushing!" Colin growled.

"Hit 'im, Mac!" someone yelled.

Colin turned to see who it was and noticed Trish sitting at her table, watching silently. His shoulders came down and his hands unclenched.

"Sorry, Mr. Cryan," he muttered. "I didn't mean it."

"Yeah, well, you just move it on down to the office!" Mr. Cryan gave him the hardest push of all, and Colin left without looking at anyone.

Trish turned back to her table, keeping her eyes down.

"Young love," someone sighed.

"Hey, Trish," Mike Pilsner called from the end of the table. "He hit you yet?"

Almost everyone laughed. Trish stuffed her lunch back into her bag, crumpling it up, getting ready to go.

"They're only kidding," Rachael said.

"Yeah, well, I don't think it's so funny." Trish got up, threw her lunch in a trash can in the front, and left the table.

Trish hung around in front of her locker after school, waiting for him.

"Trish, come on," Janet said impatiently. "Mrs. Jacobs'll kill us if we're late again today."

"I'll be right there." Trish stalled, taking books in and out of her locker.

"He's got detention, they read his name over the intercom." Janet took Trish's racket out of her locker for her. "Come on."

"I guess." Slowly, Trish spun the combination dial. "I don't feel like practicing today."

"Just come on, we're really late."

Trish let out a long, resigned sigh and followed her down the hall, stopping when she saw a familiar slouching figure.

"Tell Mrs. Jacobs I'm on my way," she said.

"Whatever." Janet continued past Colin; they nodded slightly at each other.

"Hi," Trish said.

"Hi." He moved his hands into his pockets. "You mad at me?"

"Why would I be?"

"Avoided you all day, embarrassed the hell out of you at lunch. That kind of junk."

"Oh. Well, I'm not."

"Yeah, sure." He leaned up against a locker, jamming his hands down further.

"Um, do you get in trouble if you're late?"

"What, to detention?" He shook his head. "What can they do but suspend me?" He looked up. "Why do you want to hang around me, anyway?" He moved his jaw. "Look, Trish, I like you and everything, but—"

"But what?"

"You know what people think about a girl who'd go out with me."

"I don't care."

"They'll think you sleep around."

She considered that, then shifted her weight onto one leg and put her hand on her hip.

"Maybe I do." She tossed her hair back.

"Yeah, right." He had to laugh. "You're as virgin as—I don't know. As virgin as Mary."

"That's what you think—big boy." Trish flipped her hair again.

"No way." He shook his head. "I can tell by how you walk."

She flushed, taking her normal pose.

"You can?" she asked.

"No." He grinned. "But I had to say it."

"Oh, God." She was still worried. "Can boys really tell?"

"No, they just talk a lot."

"Yeah, they do," she nodded, suddenly serious.

"Maybe you ought to remember that a lot of people just talk a lot."

He looked at her, trying to keep from smiling, trying and not succeeding.

"You're cute," he said, smiling. "And like I said, even cuter when you blush." He touched her cheek with the back of his hand. "You better get moving to tennis, woman."

"You better get moving to detention, Mac."

"Yes, ma'am." He saluted.

They smiled at each other, then started down the hall in opposite directions. Trish stopped after a few feet, turning around.

"Hey, McNamara!" she called.

"What?"

She snapped her fingers.

"Get over here," she said.

"Yes, ma'am!" He ran over, pretending to be cowed.

She threw her arms around his neck and gave him a long kiss. When they broke apart, he grinned at her.

"Virgin," he said.

"It really shows?"

"Yeah." He lifted her hand and kissed it. "What time you get out of practice?"

"Four-thirty."

"I'll be waiting." He gave her hand a squeeze, then started down the hall to detention.

Trish ran into her mother in the front hall.

"Hi." She dropped her books almost on the front table. "Where you going?"

"To pick up some groceries." Mrs. Masters pulled on a blazer. "Feel like keeping me company?"

"Um, well . . ." Trish looked toward the kitchen and the glass of orange juice—Tab?—she'd been looking forward to all afternoon.

"Of course, you do." Her mother opened the door. "Come on."

Without thinking much about it, Trish followed.

"I'm glad I didn't ask you to come jump off the John Hancock Building with me." Mrs. Masters checked to see if there were any cars coming before she crossed to the bench-lined mall. "How was school?"

"Gross."

"What about practice?"

"Okay. We only have two matches left."

"Your father and I are coming to that last home one."

"We've got a chance to win," Trish said, grinning. "I hear they've been having flu."

"Terrific."

"What did you do today?"

"Wonderful things." Her mother gestured expansively with one arm. "Freud and I went on a walk, I got to type my paper for class tonight—it's been a day to remember."

"Well, that's good." Trish's voice was serious.

Her mother smiled, giving her a one-armed hug without breaking her stride. Trish smiled back, not sure why her mother was amused.

"Hey, Mom?" she asked.

"What?"

"You thought Dad was a jerk when you first met him, right?"

"I still do sometimes."

"No, no." Trish shook her head. "I'm serious."

"Oh, I see." Her mother smiled. "Yes, I thought he was a jerk."

"He was that drunk?"

"Drunker."

"Wow." Trish thought about that. "What was the first thing he ever said to you?"

" 'Hey, you're beautiful. Wanna dance?' " Mrs. Masters laughed. "You've heard this a thousand times."

"Yeah, but I like it. Tell me again."

"Well," her mother paused at the curb, yanking Trish back out of the street, "I was at this party, and he was trying to get me to dance—I didn't even know who he was. He tried to pull me out onto the floor and managed to rip my sleeve off. Oh, cross." She pulled her daughter across the street as the signals changed. "Anyway, the next thing I knew, he was in my dorm the next day with flowers and six packages."

"Yeah? And what was in them?" Trish asked.

"You know perfectly well what was in them." Mrs. Masters smiled at her. "Six brand-new shirts." She paused. "I always wondered why he got six. I mean, why not five? Or four? Or—well, anyway, he asked me out and the next thing you knew, we were getting married."

"And then I was born," Trish prompted.

"No." They crossed Boylston Street toward the supermarket. "You were born and *then* we got married."

"Oh, funny," Trish said.

"You don't believe me? Check your birth certificate someday. Let me tell you, you were a drag on the honeymoon. Oh, wait, let me." She moved in front of her daughter to step on the rubber mat that made the supermarket door swing open automatically. "One of my simple pleasures," she explained.

"You said it, not me," Trish said, shrugging.

"Oh, my, we're being fresh today."

Trish shrugged again. "You're the one who put the plural in."

"Brat."

"Hey, can we get Tab?" Trish asked.

"No, we may not." Her mother started down the first aisle. "What do you want for dinner?"

"Steak?"

Her mother just looked at her.

"Well, you asked me what I *wanted*," Trish said.

"We could always have that tuna-fish casserole everyone likes." Mrs. Masters scanned a small, crumpled list.

"Gross."

"You don't like that casserole?" Her mother lowered the list. "You always eat it."

"I'm well brought up."

"Is that what it is?" Her mother put away the list. "Hamburger again, I guess."

"Hey, Mom?" Trish watched her pick out the freshest package.

"What?"

"Do you like Colin?"

"He seems nice enough. He doesn't talk much, though."

"He's shy." Trish put a box of cookies in the basket, and her mother took it out.

"You want cookies, you can make them," she said.

"I guess. Only they won't be like real Oreos," Trish said sadly.

"No one ever said life was easy," her mother shrugged. "Go find garlic salt, will you?"

Trish returned a minute later with the bottle.

"Everyone thinks he's a jerk." She placed the bottle in the basket.

"Who, Colin?"

"Yeah."

"Well, is he?"

"Kind of," Trish admitted. "I mean, to lots of people—not me. He's sort of flunking out."

"Sort of?"

"I guess he has mostly D's."

"Seems strange." Her mother selected a box of crackers. "I got the feeling he was pretty intelligent."

Trish nodded. "He is. Only he's got all kinds of hangups. And he's really obnoxious to teachers, so he gets sent to the office all the time."

"What's his problem?"

"I don't know. I guess he thinks he's stupid, so he won't try. It's a mess. Everyone was being really jerks about it today."

"What do you mean?"

"I don't know." Trish reached tentatively for a bag of candy bars to see if her mother was still alert. Without turning her head, Mrs. Masters took the bag out of her hand and put it back.

"How were they being jerks?" she asked, selecting one small lollipop and putting it in her daughter's hand. Trish rolled her eyes, then put it back.

"Making stupid remarks," she said. "Everyone thinks he's a sex maniac and all of that."

"Is he?" Her mother's voice was casual.

"No. They just think he is. Everyone sure was worked up about it."

"I wouldn't worry about it," Mrs. Masters said. "You know how quickly these things die down. If you like him, and he's a nice person, do you really care what everyone else thinks?"

"I guess not," Trish said uncertainly.

"Well, you shouldn't." Mrs. Masters dropped several cans of cat food into the basket. "Trish?"

"What?"

"Is he a nice person?"

"He's a nice person," Trish said.

CHAPTER ELEVEN

When Trish arrived at school on the morning of the last tennis match, she headed for her locker. As she worked her combination, she felt a hand touch her shoulder.

"Hi." It was Colin, and he was grinning at her.

"You got a haircut."

"Is it ugly?" He looked worried, his hand going up to straighten it.

"No, it looks good. I like it."

"Good." He relaxed. "Last match today, huh?"

"Yeah." Trish put her racket in the bottom of her locker.

"I'll be there." He lifted her books up to the top shelf in her locker for her.

"You will?" She tried not to sound too eager. "Y-you don't have to if you don't want to."

"Wouldn't miss it." His eyebrows leaped. "Means I get to look at you in shorts."

Trish blushed.

"Ah, first blush of the morning." He got her notebook down for her. "Come on, we'll be late for homeroom."

"Since when do you worry about being late for homeroom?"

"It's kind of fun to get there," he said. "Bradford doesn't know what to make of it. I've been bugging him all year; figured I'd give him a break." He took her books for her. "These all you have?"

"Yeah. Aren't you bringing any?"

"Nah." He shook his head. "I got horticulture first. It's a waste—all we do is sit there and watch the grass grow."

Trish laughed. "Literally?"

"Yeah. We planted these seeds, and now we sit there and watch them come up."

"Every day?"

"Yup." His expression got solemn. "Yesterday a new batch surfaced."

"No kidding? I'm sorry I missed it."

"Hey, it's your own fault you're a brain."

She reached over and squeezed his hand.

"Hey!" He jerked free. "Don't touch me in public! God, I'm so embarrassed!"

Trish's cheeks filled with color as several people stared.

"Thanks a lot," she said.

"Don't mention it." He held the door for her when they got to their homeroom.

As they walked in, a boy in the back whistled. Colin stopped, scowling, one fist doubled.

He took a threatening step in the boy's direction. "Don't even start," he warned. Including the rest of the boys in the threat with one wave of his fist, he followed Trish to her seat, pulling out her chair for her. He turned and looked at all the boys, daring them with the same doubled fist to make even one remark. No one did, and he sat down next to her.

Trish looked at Rachael, then at Colin, from her usual position in the middle.

"So," she said brightly. "Do you two know each other?"

"Hi," Colin said, a little stiff.

"Hi," Rachael said, just as stiff.

"Good." Trish nodded. "Now we're all friends."

Both Colin and Rachael snorted slightly and looked in opposite directions.

"Rachael runs two miles every morning before school," Trish went on conversationally.

"Yeah?" Colin asked with careful indifference. "Where you go?"

"Around." Rachael shrugged.

"Yeah? Me too." He flexed his right arm. "Keeps me in shape for raping, and robbing, and everything."

"Oh?" Rachael took off her glasses. "You do that a lot?"

"Yeah." He nodded. "I pillage too."

Rachael almost smiled.

"Then, like on Sunday afternoons," Colin clenched both fists, "I beat up old ladies."

"You got six last week, didn't you?" Trish asked.

"Eight," he said proudly. He looked at Rachael. "What do you do for fun?"

After homeroom, Colin walked the two girls down the hall to their trigonometry room. There outside the door, he handed Trish her books.

"Well," he said. "Gotta go watch the grass grow."

"You do that for fun too?" Rachael asked.

"All the time." Colin started down the hall. "Later."

They both watched him go.

"You don't think he's cute?" Trish asked.

"Maybe." Rachael shrugged noncommittally.

"Only maybe?" Trish grinned at her and they went into Trigonometry.

"Colin?" Miss Nelson asked him later, during reading class.

"What? Me?" He straightened up, jerking his gaze from the window.

"Don't you think you ought to pay attention?" she asked, her glasses slipping down. "We're on page forty-four."

He opened his book, still staring out the window.

She followed his eyes. "What are you looking at? There's really not much to see."

"You think it'll rain?" he asked.

"It might. Why don't you read from the top of the page?"

"If it rains, they'll, like, cancel the tennis match, won't they?"

"You mean the girls' team? I guess so." She pushed her glasses up.

"Colin's got a girl friend, Colin's got a girl friend," a boy chanted.

"Robby's gonna get his face broke, Robby's gonna get his face broke," Colin chanted back.

"How about Colin's gonna read from the top of the page?" Miss Nelson suggested.

He looked down at his book.

"Too boring," he said. "No pictures."

"There was a picture on the last page, if you'd been paying attention."

He flipped back.

"Well, will ya look at that?" he said. "A nice boy carrying groceries. Wonder if he stole them?"

"If you read, we could find out," Miss Nelson said.

"How about tomorrow?" Colin closed his book. "I, like, get into suspense." He reopened his book, turning a few pages ahead, pausing at the first picture. "And here are some scenes from our next episode." He made his voice very deep, looking at the drawing of the smiling boy in a garden. "Dickie is weeding for his mother—without even being asked—when the store detective comes and apprehents him for stealing the groceries." He looked up, "Sorry. Did I like, ruin the story for everyone?"

"It's apprehen*d*s," Miss Nelson pushed her glasses up.

Colin shook his head. "Uh-uh. My dad's a cop and I know this stuff. It's apprehen*t*s."

"Colin . . ."

"Hmmm." Colin frowned. "Or maybe it was apprehence. I forget."

"Here." Miss Nelson handed him a dictionary. "You look it up, and we'll go on with the story."

"How do I look it up if I can't spell it?"

"It begins with 'a.' "

"Thanks a lot." He opened to the first page. " 'A. The f-first le-l-letter,' " he said, sounding the word out. "The

95

first letter of the m-mod-modern al-pha—alphabet.'' He shook his head. ''I'll never find it. Too many words beginning with 'a.' ''

The bell rang, and he jumped up.

''That's it!'' he shouted. ''Take off, everyone!''

''Colin, would you stay here for a minute?'' Miss Nelson asked.

''But I'll be late for math,'' he said. ''And we can't be having that.''

''I'll write you a pass.''

He shrugged, swinging his legs back onto the table.

''What can I do you for, Miss Nelson?'' he asked.

''Colin.'' Miss Nelson took her glasses off, moving thin hair back behind her ears. ''Do you have to be so disruptive all the time? You're holding everyone back.''

''What, you mean 'cause I'm so stupid?''

''I don't think you're stupid. In fact, I know you're not. If you could just stop clowning around and get to work, I think you'd be out of here in no time.''

''But I'd miss you.'' He pretended to be close to tears.

''See?'' she asked. ''How can I help you if you won't give me a chance?''

He shrugged.

She pulled two mimeographed sheets out of a folder, handing them to him. ''I corrected your reading comprehension test from Wednesday.''

''Oh yeah?'' He scanned it. ''Hey, fifty-four! I'm moving up in the world.''

''It's a fourth-grade reading level, Colin.'' She sighed. ''I know you can do better than that.''

''No.'' He gave the papers back to her. ''My mind's Jell-O.''

She ignored that. ''Would you like to go over the passage?'' she asked. ''I can help you with the questions you didn't understand.''

''But I have math now,'' he pointed out. ''And I can't be missing math.''

For a minute, she didn't speak. Then, she dropped the test, folding her hands on top of it. "Colin, what do you want to do with your life?"

"Do?" He sat back. "I dunno. Burn libraries, I guess."

"Colin."

"Sorry. I meant, li*berries*." He stood up. "Look, Miss Nelson, I know you're, like, just trying to help, but don't bother. I'm a jerk."

"I don't think you are."

"Yeah, sure." He looked at the clock. "I'd better go bug my math teacher."

"Wait, I'll give you a pass—"

"No, he'd have a heart attack if I showed up with one." Colin put on a solemn expression. "And we can't be having that." He paused at the door. "You know, I'm doing pretty good in reading—I'm on a *third*-grade level in math." He flashed the smile and left.

Warming up for her singles match that afternoon, Trish kept glancing around to see if Colin had come yet. She saw Rachael sitting with a bunch of other juniors. Her parents were also in the crowd and they waved. She waved back, returning to her warm-up.

"You want to take some serves?" her opponent called.

"What? Oh, I guess." She took a few balls and went back to the baseline, hitting three—none of which went in; she didn't even notice her opponent's growing air of confidence with every missed shot.

Right before they started to play, Trish went back to the fence to wipe her racket with a towel. Her father came over.

"What's wrong with you?" he asked, leaning against the chain links. "Your form's terrible. I don't think you're even looking at the ball."

"My concentration's sort of off," she admitted.

"Is it making you nervous that we're here?"

"No." She shook her head. "I'm glad."

"Well, come on. You can beat this girl."

"I guess."

"She stands over too far, she's guarding her backhand. Move her around."

"I guess."

He frowned, still convinced that she was nervous because they had come.

"Pretend we're not here, okay?" he asked.

"Okay." She turned back to the court to see her coach, who handed her three new balls.

"Who won service?" Mrs. Jacobs asked.

"Me."

"Try and get her backhand."

"Yeah."

The coach frowned. "Do you feel okay?"

"Yeah."

"Well, we're counting on you. You, Janet, and Heidi should all win. That way, if we only take one doubles match, we can still win. Wouldn't it be nice to win?"

"Yeah." Trish nodded, seeing in one quick look that Colin still hadn't come. "I know. Don't worry, I'll try."

"Okay. Work her backhand."

Trish nodded again, shoving one ball in her pocket, holding the other two.

"You ready?" she called to her opponent.

The girl nodded.

"These're good." Trish threw the ball up and served.

"Long," the girl said as the ball skipped out.

Trish frowned, throwing the second ball up. It was three o'clock. Where was he?

"Long," the girl said, hitting both balls back.

Trish caught them, moving to the other side of the baseline, trying to force herself to concentrate. He forgot, that was all. Or something happened. Don't worry about it. She served again.

"Long," the girl said.

Trish served the next one gently and it went into the net.

"Love–thirty," she muttered.

"Concentrate," Mrs. Jacobs said from the fence.

"I know." Trish finally got one in, but missed the girl's returned shot. "Love–forty." Concentrate, will you?

She lost the first three games easily.

"You're much better than she is," Mrs. Jacobs said from the fence.

Trish winced and bent down to receive service, deciding to give up on him and pay attention to her game. The first serve came at her and she aimed at the girl's backhand, but hit the ball out of bounds. She lost that game too, and stood behind the baseline, bouncing a ball, ignoring her opponent's confident stance on the other side of the net.

Come on, she told herself, you're ten times better than she is. Forget it; he's not coming, he's a jerk. Just forget it. She turned to check the spectators one more time, and saw Colin hurrying toward the courts. He waved, and she waved back, relaxing. She spun around to serve, knocking the first ball in like a cannonball for an easy ace. Moving to the other side to serve again, she checked to make sure he really was there, and hit another ace. Mrs. Jacobs followed Trish's gaze to see a boy in a flannel shirt leaning up against a car, hands in his pockets, watching the courts. She sighed; if only he'd gotten there twenty minutes earlier.

Trish won the next six games in a row, taking the first set. Her opponent moved back to the baseline, rather dazed, to confer with her coach. Trish went to get her towel to wipe off her racket, and saw Colin coming over.

"I can see my being here makes you nervous," he said.

"Yeah," she nodded. "Go away, will you?"

"I'm sorry I was late. I sort of had detention."

"It's okay. I just thought you forgot."

"Never. I really wanted to come." He gestured toward the other side of the net. "She looks kind of dizzy."

Trish shrugged. "I guess she thought she had an easy win. I played pretty lousy the first few games."

"I heard someone saying you double-faulted, like, six times."

"Only five," she said. "I guess I wasn't concentrating." She lowered her voice, leaning closer. "Don't leave, okay?"

"I promise. And I'm really sorry I was late, I didn't mean to be." He touched her hand through the fence. "I'm rooting for you, woman."

Six games later, Trish won the match.

CHAPTER TWELVE

The team still lost, even though Trish and Janet won their matches.

"I heard you decided to give everyone a scare," Janet said as she and Trish walked toward the spectators.

"Yeah," Trish agreed. "It took me a while to get warmed up."

"Hi." Colin came over to meet them, proud eyes fixed on Trish. "You guys were both really good."

"Thanks," Trish said as Janet nodded. "Janet, you know Colin, right?"

"Yeah," Janet said.

There was a short, awkward silence.

Janet broke it. "I'd better go. I'll talk to you tomorrow, Trish."

"Right," Trish said. "Have a good time tonight."

Janet made her hands tremble and kept going.

"God," Colin said, shaking his head. "Your friends really like me."

"She's just nervous. She's going out with Peter Cameron tonight. Do you know him?"

Colin shrugged. "He's in my gym class." His eyes darted up and down. "You look really pretty."

"Oh, thank you," she said, shy.

"Can I kiss you?"

"Not in front of all these people."

He glanced around. "What people?"

"People like them," she said, pointing at her parents, who were approaching.

"You gave us a turn," Mrs. Masters said. "Your father and I were afraid we were making you nervous. Hi, Colin."

"Hi, Mrs. Masters, hi, Mr. Masters." Colin pulled his hands out of his pockets.

"Did you enjoy the match?" Trish's father asked.

"Yes, sir, very much. Your daughter's a very good player."

"Yes," Mr. Masters agreed, "when she concentrates. Do you want a ride home, Trish, or is the team going out?"

"Mrs. Jacobs is having a party next week for everyone," Trish said. "I just have to go in and get my books; I'll be right out."

"I'll carry your racket for you," Colin offered.

She smiled and handed it to him.

"It was nice seeing you again, Mr. and Mrs. Masters," he said politely before following Trish back to the school.

"It was nice seeing you too, Colin," Mrs. Masters said.

Trish took her racket back when they got to the locker room.

"So, I'll be by at seven," Colin said.

"Okay. I'm glad you came."

"I'm glad too." He checked the hall and saw that it was empty. "*Now* can I kiss you?"

She put her racket down and lifted her arms up onto his shoulders and they embraced for a long minute.

"Mmm," he said, pulling his head away. "Can I come by around six?"

She laughed and hugged him.

"You know—" he rested his hands on her waist—"you do look awfully pretty. Can I give you another kiss?"

"Sure," she said.

Colin scowled into his closet, then kicked the door shut. He threw open his dresser drawers, rifled through the clothes, and scowling harder, slammed the drawers shut.

"This is awful, cat!" He took Ophelia off the top of the dresser where she'd been sitting watching him, and sat grumpily down on his bed to pat her.

"What's wrong?" his mother asked from the door, holding a bag.

"I have nothing to wear." He kicked his bedpost. "She always looks so pretty."

She handed him the bag. "I bought you a present today."

His eyes lit up as he pulled out a green-and-white-striped shirt.

"Hey, button-down and everything!" He stared at the shirt. "Pretty wild!"

"I thought you might want to go shopping this weekend." She touched the faded collar of his flannel shirt. "Maybe we could go get some other new things?"

"It costs too much money."

"Not that much."

He was still staring at the shirt.

"Wow, thanks." He hugged her. "This is really great."

"It'll bring out your eyes." She tried to fix his hair. "So, am I a pretty wild mother?"

"I don't know." He grinned. "You tell me. I know you're a pretty great mother. I'm not so sure about wild."

"Get dressed," she laughed. "You don't want to be late to pick her up."

"You're right, I don't." He started to unbutton his shirt.

When he was ready to go, his parents were both in the living room, watching the news. His father glanced up.

"Well, lad, you're looking sharp," he said.

"You think?" Colin straightened his collar, making his voice a little deeper than usual.

"He's a looker," Mrs. McNamara said.

"Do you have plenty of money?" Colin's father reached into his back pocket for his wallet. "You want ten dollars?"

"I'm all set," Colin assured him. "Thanks anyway. I'd better get going."

"Have a good time," his mother said. "It's getting colder, you'd better take a sweater."

"Okay. I won't be late."

His father sniffed, smelling after-shave.

"I didn't know you'd started shaving, lad," he said.

"Oh." Colin flushed. "Uh, well, I guess I sort of haven't. I gotta go, I'm late." He hurried out to the door, grabbing his dark-green sweater off the coatrack on the way.

Greg answered the door.

"Hi," Colin said. "Your sister here?"

"Yeah, c'mon in."

Colin stepped into the hall, closing the door behind him.

"I'll go get her." Greg's eyes sparkled. "She's been getting dressed for about twenty hours."

Colin nodded. "Always figured she was slow."

Mrs. Masters came out as Greg went upstairs.

"Hi, Colin. Oh, you look very nice."

"Thanks." Colin straightened his collar again. "Don't worry, I'll have her home early."

"I know," Mrs. Masters assured him. "Although parents always worry."

"Yeah, mine sure do," he agreed. "Mom always waits up. Dad says he doesn't, but he usually shows up in my room to ask if I had a good time." He shook his head. "They're pretty wild."

"I hope I get to meet them."

"Yeah, you'd like them." He leaned against the banister, relaxing. "Maybe you could talk my mother into going back to school. Trish said you did."

"I'm really enjoying it." Mrs. Masters sat down on the chair next to the front hall table, also relaxing. "I wish I'd done it five years ago."

"What are you studying?"

"Well, I'm trying to get my masters'—"

"Isn't every degree you get a Masters degree?" he asked.

"I guess it is," she laughed. "I'll be getting it in drama, mostly theater history. I don't know what I'm going to do with it, but I'm enjoying the courses."

"Drama's wonderful." Colin's eyes glowed. "Who's your favorite playwright?"

"It's hard to choose." Mrs. Masters focused on the wallpaper, thinking. "Wilson, Albee, Giraudoux—they're all so different. Who's yours?"

"Well, Shakespeare—but everyone. Did you see *Who's Afraid of Virginia Woolf?* the other night? It was the late movie."

"Isn't it wonderful?" Mrs. Masters put on a solemn expression. " 'What a dump.' "

"I keep practicing that Requiem for the Dead—you know the part?" he asked. " 'Libera me, Domine, de morte aeterna, in die illa tremenda' "—God, talk about breath control. I'll probably never get it down."

"Are you interested in acting?"

"Yeah." His eyes were still far away, back in his room where he practiced so faithfully, practiced for the invisible audience. "I'd love to be an actor."

"Did you and Trish meet in the drama club?"

"Huh?" His eyes came back to the hall. "You mean, at school? No, I'm not in it."

"Trish was telling me that there aren't too many boys involved. You could probably get some good parts."

"I don't know, I'm not so good." He shrugged. "Besides, they're all pretty—"

"Hi." Trish hurried down the stairs. "Sorry I took so long, I had to brush my teeth. Oh, you look nice, Colin."

"Thanks." He straightened his collar. "So do you."

"Hey," Mrs. Masters said, looking at her watch. "If you two are going to make the movie, you'd better get going."

"Yeah." Colin helped Trish into her blazer. "It was nice talking to you, Mrs. Masters. *Streetcar Named Desire* is on tomorrow, you know."

"Oh, really? Terrific," she said. "Maybe I can get Ben away from football. Have a good time, you two."

"We will," Trish said. "And don't worry, I won't be late."

"Who worries?" Mrs. Masters asked.

Colin paused at the door.

" 'The game is five-card stud,' " he said.

" 'I have always depended on the kindness of strangers,' " Mrs. Masters countered.

"Way to go," he said. "Later." He held the door for Trish and they went outside.

"That's a great movie," Trish said as they crossed the street.

"Yeah, I love it," he agreed, eyes distant again. "Hey, you wanna watch it at my house? You can meet my parents and everything!" He didn't give her time to answer. "Yeah, great. They wanna meet you. And we can watch the movie and—it's perfect!"

"What if they hate me?" Trish asked nervously.

"We'll put you in a cab and send you home." He pulled her over, kissing her on the top of the head. "I can't wait." He hugged her. "You smell wonderful! Let's go to the movie!"

"Okay." She laughed and slipped her arm through his. "In a good mood tonight?"

"I'm in a wonderful mood!" He started singing "On the Street Where You Live," his voice deep and masculine. He checked both ways, then danced her across the street.

"Hey, you have a good voice," she said, leaning back in his arms as they got to the other side of the street.

"You think?" He shook his head. "I just play around. Come on." He kept one arm around her. "We don't want to miss this thing."

After the movie they sat in Brigham's for half an hour with drinks and a shared order of French fries. Then they walked down Commonwealth Avenue slowly, savoring the night.

"It's so quiet," she whispered.

"Yeah." He glanced at the town houses, silent but warmed by the glow of light on red brick. "It's beautiful." He saw her house up ahead. "You, uh, you have to go in right away?"

"I don't know. It's still pretty early, isn't it?"

They kept walking down the path, Colin pausing in front

of a statue of a soldier caught with one knee out in the middle of a brave stride forward.

"John Glover," he said. "Wonder what he was like?"

"Pugnacious," Trish guessed.

"Probably." He glanced over at a tree-shadowed bench. "You wanna sit down?"

"Sure."

They sat down and he put his arm around her.

"Mmmm," he inhaled. "You really do smell good."

"English Leather," she said.

"Who, you?"

"No, you."

"Yeah." He brought his free hand up to her cheek. "Is it okay if I kiss you?"

"You have to ask?"

He laughed. "My father says it's good manners."

"Oh. Well, then, yeah, it's okay."

He bent his head to meet hers and they moved closer together.

"Do I do this right?" she asked against his mouth.

"I love the way you do it." He kissed her nose, then her eyebrows. "Am I okay?"

"You're okay."

They kept kissing, sometimes talking, sometimes not. His breathing came faster, and his hand slid from her back to her lower rib cage.

"Uh." He kept his hand on her waist. "You mind if I do this?"

"Well," she said uncertainly, "what if someone walks by?"

"Then they'll think we're awfully bad."

"What if it's my father or someone?"

"Then he'll probably hit me." Colin kissed her. "It's okay if you mind."

"It's not that, it's just—" She blushed. "I haven't gone out with very many guys."

"So?"

"Well." She shifted on the bench. "I haven't done much."

"I know."

"Does it matter?"

"Trish," he held her face with both hands, "all that matters is that you tell me if I do something you don't want me to do, okay?"

She nodded.

"Good." He pulled her close, very gently kissing her hair.

"Colin?"

"What?" He kissed her ear.

"Is it," she hesitated, "*normal* to be my age and not to have done much?"

"Well, I don't know," he said seriously. "How old are you?"

"Colin!" She pushed him. "I mean it."

"Sure it's normal. What do you think?"

"I don't know." She picked up his hand, playing with it. "Sometimes I get the feeling there's something wrong with me."

"Of course there isn't." He kissed her cheek. "So you haven't done much. Big deal."

"Is it normal," she concentrated on his hand, "to be—I don't know—scared about things?"

"Things like sex?"

She blushed and nodded.

"Sure, who isn't? It's a pretty big deal. Look—" he hugged her—"just promise you won't ever be scared around me, okay? We'll do whatever you want."

"What both of us want," Trish said.

He smiled. "What both of us want," he agreed.

CHAPTER THIRTEEN

"Are you sure I look all right?" Trish asked nervously, outside Colin's brownstone the next night.

"You look beautiful," he assured her. "I love your pink pants."

"You've never seen them before; I haven't worn them in weeks."

He grinned. "I've seen them. What do you think—I never looked at you before?"

"I don't know."

"I looked at you a lot. He studied her for a second. "Yeah, you look good. Besides, don't worry; they'll love you." He opened the door, leading her inside. "Mom? Dad?"

His parents came out: Mr. McNamara, big and friendly, looking like his son, in a gray V-neck sweater; Mrs. McNamara, small and fluttery, in a dark-green dress.

"Mom, Dad, this is Trish." Colin rested a nervous hand on her back. "Trish, these are my parents."

"H-hi." Trish's smile was weak.

Mr. McNamara grinned and took her arm.

"We've heard a lot about you. Come in and sit down," he said. "Would you be liking a drink?"

"I don't drink," Trish said hastily.

"I meant a Coke," he explained. "Or whatever you like."

"Oh," she said.

"I bought some Tab," Colin said, following his mother into the kitchen to help.

"Come on." Mr. McNamara brought Trish into the living room, gesturing for her to sit down.

109

She lowered herself onto the edge of the couch, neatly crossing her ankles, while he sat in an easy chair perpendicular to her. She glanced around at the quiet, comfortable furniture; the shelves cluttered with worn books; the small black-and-white cat sprawled out in front of a feeble fire.

"We'll have to get Colin to fix that up," Mr. McNamara said, gesturing toward the fire. "He's the only one around here who can do it." He smiled at her. "You know, if you were wanting wine or something, you could have it."

"No, thank you."

"I'm glad we're finally seeing you," he said. "Colin never stops talking about you."

"He's always telling me about both of you," Trish said shyly.

Mr. McNamara grinned. "He's a loyal lad. If he decides he likes someone, they're usually stuck with him."

"I don't mind." Trish's voice was even more shy.

Mrs. McNamara carried a tray in, Colin following her with his awkward what-do-I-do-with-my-hands-if-I-don't-put-them-in-my-pockets walk. She put the tray down on the low table in front of the couch, then handed Trish her Tab, with a napkin underneath the glass.

"Thank you," Trish said.

Mr. McNamara took his coffee and reached for the sugar bowl, knocking the spoon out and onto the floor. All three McNamaras looked at it, then at Trish, who hesitated, her glass halfway to her mouth.

"What?" she asked.

"Nothing at all." Mrs. McNamara hurriedly picked the spoon up.

"It means a child's coming," Colin explained, taking his glass of Coke and sitting next to her on the couch.

Trish gulped, still holding her glass in midair.

"And it's just a silly superstition," Mrs. McNamara said briskly. "Only fools believe in them; I don't give them a second thought."

Colin and Mr. McNamara raised eyebrows at her.

"Well, I don't," she said.

The doorbell rang and she jumped up to answer it. The three in the living room heard her open the door; then a small voice piped, "My mother wanted to know if we could borrow a cup of sugar, Mrs. McNamara?"

"Thanks be to God, and you can have two!" she exclaimed.

In the living room, Colin laughed.

"But she doesn't believe in superstitions," he said.

Mrs. McNamara returned to the living room, beaming.

"See?" She looked at her husband. "They never fail." Smiling, she sat down with her coffee.

"Colin tells us you're a tennis player," Mr. McNamara said.

"I'm not very good," Trish said.

"Oh, you should have seen her the other day." Colin brushed his hand across hers. "She won her match in twelve straight games! She hit about ten aces!"

"Only eight," Trish corrected him. "I was just lucky. I think the girl I was playing had the flu."

"Colin also mentioned that you're full of confidence," Mr. McNamara said wryly.

Trish nodded. "That's why we like each other."

His parents laughed.

"Think I'll see what I can do with the fire." Colin got up, patted Ophelia, and moved the fire screen out of the way.

"What do you think you want to do when you get out of school, Trish?" Mrs. McNamara asked.

"I don't really know," Trish admitted. "I mean, college, I guess, but after that, I'm not sure. I think about law, but who knows?"

"That's for sure." Mr. McNamara looked at his son.

"What time is it?" Colin finished fixing the fire abruptly. "We don't want to miss the beginning of the movie."

"Almost eight," Mrs. McNamara checked her watch.

Colin flipped on the television and turned to the right

channel. Sitting down, he glanced at the leaping fire. Ophelia jumped into his lap and he stroked her back.

"Think I'll be an arsonist when I grow up," he said.

When the movie was over, he stretched; Ophelia stretched too.

"You wanna see my room?" he asked Trish. "I'm kind of, like, a master decorator."

"I can imagine." Trish hesitated, eyes on the tray. "Mrs. McNamara, would you like me to—?"

"I'll take care of it," Colin's mother assured her. "Thank you, though."

When they got down the hall, he threw open his door.

"My boudoir," he said.

She grinned. "Maybe I'll just wait out here."

"Nope."

She started to say something as they went inside, but suddenly he jumped on her, forcing her across the room and onto his bed.

"My God, what are you doing?" she gasped, staring up at him.

"I'm attacking you!"

"I knew you were an animal." She sat up, straightening her hair. She scanned the room, taking in the overcrowded bookshelves and the haphazard pile of paperbacks on his desk. "If your teachers could see you now."

He shuddered. "Thank God they can't."

"Marilyn's very nice," she said.

"You think?" He grinned at his poster. "I can say I sleep with her anyway, right?"

"Your father said you practice scenes in here." She flipped through the copy of *Barefoot in the Park* next to his bed.

"When'd he say that?" Colin idly kicked his bedpost.

"When you went out of the room."

"Well, yeah, maybe sometimes." He shrugged.

"He said all the time."

"Well, maybe." Colin kicked the post again. "I don't know."

"Would you do one?"

"What, now?" His head jerked up.

"Why not?"

"I don't know, I don't feel like it." He backed up toward the door.

"Not even one?"

"I don't want to!" He backed up more. "Leave me alone!"

"Okay." Trish put the book down, her expression stiff. "I'm sorry."

"Oh, great." He let his breath out. "You mad now?"

"You're asking *me*?"

"Yeah, you're right." He sat down on the bottom of the bed. "Guess I get kind of paranoid."

"I know."

"Guess you do." He nodded.

She moved over and ran her hand through his hair.

"If you could have any part in the world, who would you be?" she asked.

"I don't know."

His shoulders didn't relax; she squeezed the muscles.

"It should be something where you can sing." She squeezed harder. "I love your voice."

"You do?"

"It's *really* sexy."

"It is?" He rubbed an experimental hand down his throat, then pitched his voice very low. "Do, re, mi, fa, so, la, ti, do."

"Oh, God." Trish fell back on the bed. "You're too sexy."

"You think?" He bent over her, making his voice even lower. "Do, ti, la, so, fa, mi, re, do."

"Oh!" She pretended to pass out. "Please, stop!"

Someone cleared his throat and they looked up to see Mr. McNamara.

113

"Uh, hi." Colin coughed. "This, uh, this must look pretty bad."

"I'd agree with you there. I'm sorry, I didn't mean to be interrupting you." He brought one eyebrow down in a frown. "Colin, watch yourself."

"Yes, sir," he said meekly.

Mr. McNamara nodded and left the room.

"I should have figured he'd come check." Colin ran his hand through his hair. "He worries a lot."

"Now, they'll hate me," Trish groaned.

"No, they won't." He threw his arms around her, forcing her back down. "Come on, let's give him something to really look at!"

"Colin, cut it out," she said, squirming free. Still red, she moved over to the bookcase. "Uh, did you like *The Jungle?*"

"Not as much as I liked *The Scarlet Letter*." He grinned.

Trish ignored that. "Did you get all the way through *Moby Dick*?" she asked.

"Yeah. It was a fight, though."

"What about *Absalom, Absalom*?"

"No one's perfect." He shrugged. "*The Sound and the Fury* was pretty wild, though."

"What are you getting in reading?"

"I have a sixty-three average," he said.

She shook her head, turning away from the bookcase.

"Could you do something for me?"

"Maybe." He kicked his bedpost.

"It's important."

"I said, maybe."

"Could you tell your teacher the truth? Just in that one class? Could you do that for me?"

"Why for you?" he asked stiffly. "It's my own stupid business."

"Because you won't do it for you. Do you like me enough to do it for me?"

He shrugged.

"I, uh—" She swallowed. "I like you that much."

"Oh, God." He kicked his bedpost.

"Please?"

"I don't know; maybe."

She sighed and turned back to the bookcase.

"What did you think of *To Kill a Mockingbird?*" she asked.

After he walked her home, Colin came into the apartment very quietly, hoping his father was alseep.

"Colin?" his father called.

"Yeah?"

"Come in here."

Colin winced and went into the living room, where his father was reading *Time*.

"Where's Mom?"

"She went to bed already." Mr. McNamara put down his magazine. "We both liked her; she seems like a nice girl."

"She is," Colin agreed. "I'm pretty tired, think I'll go to bed."

"I thought we could talk for a minute." His father gestured toward the couch. "Sit down, lad."

Colin sat down, and neither of them said anything for a minute.

"What do you want to talk about?" Colin asked.

"I thought we could talk about sex."

"What about it?"

"About having it, I guess." Mr. McNamara shifted in his chair. "There was a time when I was young, lad, and I know how you must be feeling."

"You're not old."

"I guess it depends on your definition," his father said. Besides, I think I was talking about control. It's harder when you're young. You look at a girl; you might be a little in love with her, and—" He shrugged again.

"What are you saying?" Colin's arms went across his chest.

"What I'm saying, lad, is that your mother and I were young once. All I'd do would be look at her, and—well, I don't mind telling you that it wasn't the easiest period in my life. For control, I mean. Of course, it was one of the happiest periods in my life too, when I'm thinking about it." He frowned, wondering if he'd gotten too far off the track. "Colin, d'you have any questions?"

"Didn't we do this when I was twelve?"

"Yeah, but you weren't liking a girl then." He looked at his son. "I don't want you to run into problems. Y've had your share."

Colin didn't say anything.

"So—" his father moved over next to him—"how're things going with her?"

"Fine."

"And you like her a lot?"

"I guess."

"Colin, don't be shutting off on me, I hate that." His father spoke quietly, but Colin winced, recognizing the hurt and irritation.

"I'm not shutting off. It's just—" He shook his head.

"I like her looks," Mr. McNamara said. "I've never been one to go after the blondes—thinking your mother's the most beautiful woman in the world—but your girl, I like her looks."

"Me too."

"She's nice. What you've been needing is someone nice." He frowned. "And you don't want to talk about sex?"

"It is kind of hard," Colin admitted. "It's, like, I walked her to class the other day and before she went in, she sort of touched my hand. I thought I was gonna die. I, like, quit smoking, but I went to the guys' bathroom and bummed two off Nicky Parillo." He glanced up, embarrassed. "Did that ever happen to you?"

"Are you kidding, lad?" His father sat back. "I was seventeen once too."

"Did it ever happen in front of them?"

"All the time."

"What'd you do?"

His father shrugged. "Run away. What else?"

Colin laughed, and sat back too. "Can they tell what you're thinking?" he asked.

"What do you mean?"

"I mean, like, if you're thinking about it." Colin put his hands behind his head. "I try not to look at her, I figure she'd be embarrassed. Only, I always want to. Sometimes I kind of walk a little behind her, so she can't tell."

"Y've inherited good blood, lad," Mr. McNamara said.

"You should see her walk." Colin stared at the dying fire. "It's not like she moves all around, or wears tight clothes, or anything. It's just—I don't know. I like to watch her."

His father grinned. "Y've inherited good taste too, lad."

"You know how Ophelia walks?" Colin glanced at the little cat asleep on the rug. "The way her muscles kind of flow along and it's just part of it? Trish does that. It's like she—" He stopped, straightening up. "But don't worry, I've got control."

"I hope so."

"Hell, yes. As long as she doesn't walk, and I don't look at her, I'm fine."

"That's good to hear." His father's voice was wry.

"No, really." Colin grew serious. "All I've really done is kiss her. I think I'm practically the first guy who's even done that to her. I'm really careful—I ask permission and stuff."

"Y've got to have good manners," Mr. McNamara agreed.

"That's what I told her. So don't worry. I'm fine as long as I don't look at her, or think about her." Colin's eyebrows jumped mischievously.

"Well, just remember: control, lad. Key word there."

"Control." Colin nodded. "I'll watch myself."

"You do that," his father said.

CHAPTER FOURTEEN

Colin went to classes the next couple of days, behaving the way he always did. Trish hadn't mentioned anything about reading class again, although she'd looked at him funny a couple of times. So, he just sort of conveniently forgot she'd ever said anything; it was easier that way. Safer.

On Thursday, he slouched low in his chair, book closed.

"Colin?" Miss Nelson asked, her voice hopeful.

"Huh?" He looked up. "What?"

"We're having another diagnostic test Friday. Why don't you go over the reading lists with the rest of us?"

"Too boring," he said. "I'd just as soon sit here."

"Well," she pushed her glasses up, "that's sort of the easy way out, isn't it?"

"Yeah, probably."

"You won't at least try?"

Colin slouched lower.

"Come on, Colin. Why don't you read us the first five—"

"Hey, I get lots of reading done in *Playboy*," he said. "Like the articles are really good, y'know?" He grinned as the others laughed. "Everyone says so." He looked at Miss Nelson, her eyes on thin hands, twisting the ring around her fourth finger. He wondered when she'd gotten it. Had to have been recently. She was pretty young when you looked at her, like maybe right out of college. He should probably stop bugging her. Restless as they went on with the word lists, he stood up, slouching over to the bookcase.

"Colin?" she asked. "Do you want something?"

He smiled benignly.

"Just pretend I'm not here." He frowned at the books as if he couldn't even read any of the titles.

She went on with the class and he arbitrarily selected a book. Suddenly, perversely, he decided that Trish was right, that doing all of this was really stupid, that he was sick of it.

"What's this?" He held up the book.

"It's a book," she answered, "by William Faulkner."

The class was watching now, word lists forgotten.

"L-Li—oh, Light!" Colin sounded the first word out. "Light in—Au-gust. Light in August!" His expression got sad. "Like maybe someday, I can be reading this?"

"If you pay attention now."

He had to grin: she'd almost gotten him.

"No, no, I want to read this." He flipped the book open. "Oh, yeah, chapter six. This was, like, my favorite part."

"Colin." She spoke patiently. "Why don't you come sit down?"

"What?" His eyebrows shot up and he took a backward step. "Discouraging me from reading?"

Her lips came together; he'd won that one.

"I'll just read a little." He squinted at the page. "M-mem—ory. Memor-y, memory! Yeah, memory. Memory believes be-before—wait a minute. Memory believes before—" He frowned at the next word. "K-k—now—ing. Now what is that supposed to be?"

"Knowing," Miss Nelson said quietly. "The 'k' is silent."

"Oh, yeah, yeah, now I remember. Memory—hey, kind of funny, I *remember* my *memory*?"

Everyone laughed but Miss Nelson.

"Anyway, where was I? Memory believes before knowing remem-oh, remembers!" His eyes lit up. "How about that? Look, I was just saying that and here it is!" He shook his head. "Small world, huh?"

"Come on, Colin, why don't you sit down?" Miss Nelson suggested, her fragile look fading to a before-tears look.

"Okay, okay, one more sec." He didn't notice, staring at the page. " 'Memory believes before knowing remembers.' Whatever that's supposed to mean." He glanced up to see the before-tears look and felt very guilty. "Okay, okay, one more quick sentence." He scanned the group, seeing that he had their full attention, seeing that this was the perfect time to jump in. Lifting the book, he arched his eyebrows just enough to create an expression of wry, self-deprecating superiority, clearing his throat. He spoke in his deep orating voice, in a measured, winding rhythm; the way the words had been written, the way they were meant to be spoken. " 'Believes longer than recollects, longer than knowing even wonders. Knows remembers believes a corridor in a big long garbled cold echoing building of dark red brick soot-bleakened by more chimneys than its own, set in a grassless cinderstrewnpacked compound surrounded by smoking factory purlieus and enclosed by a ten foot steel-and-wire fence like a penitentiary or a zoo, where in random erratic surges, with sparrowlike, childtrebling orphans in identical and uniform blue denim in and out of remembering, but in knowing constant as the bleak walls, the bleak windows where in rain soot from the yearly adjacenting chimneys streaked like black tears.' " He paused. "It was the sort of 'tale told by an idiot, full of sound and fury, yet signifying—nothing.' "

In the silence that followed, he slapped the book shut, noisily taking his place.

"Sorry, Miss Nelson." He bent over his word list. "Guess I'm being kind of disruptive today, huh?"

She went on with the class without a word, but at the end, pushed her word list away.

"Would you mind staying after for a minute, Mr. McNamara?" she asked.

"I can't be missing math all the time, ma'am."

"I think you can stay today."

He returned to his seat, grinning hugely; Miss Nelson waited until the others left.

"I guess you were right when you said you were a jerk," she said.

He just grinned.

"Would you come here for a second?" She walked over to the shelves. When he got there, she gestured to a row. "What, out of these, haven't you read?"

"Well," he skimmed the titles. "*Little Women*. I couldn't get through that Marmie stuff, or Marmsie, or whatever it was they called her." He kept going down the line. "Never heard of *The Glory Tent*. Oh, and *Ivanhoe*. I gotta be honest, I didn't finish it."

"Good God." Miss Nelson looked at the books. "On that shelf alone, you've probably read more than any junior honors student in the school."

He shook his head. "Not Trish. I bet she read *Little Women*."

"Trish?"

"Just a girl I know."

Miss Nelson nodded.

"Colin." She sat back down at the table. "How long have you been able to read?"

"Dunno." He put his hands in his pockets. "Since I was about eight, I guess."

"Are you pulling this same kind of stuff in all your other classes?"

"Guess so."

"Why?"

"I don't know." He didn't look at her, his hands going deeper into his pockets. "I guess I'm stupid."

"I think the last thing you are is stupid."

"Yeah, but I flunk everything."

"Have you ever heard of test anxiety?" she asked.

"Yeah, I guess."

"It happens to a lot of people. They get into exams and they freeze. Even if they know the answers, they can't usually put them down."

Colin shrugged. "Sounds like a bunch of pretty stupid people."

"It happens to me," Miss Nelson said. "My SAT's and GRE's were terrible."

"But I thought you went to Wesleyan and all."

"I did. Test results aren't everything." She folded her arms. "It's one of the reasons I decided to teach reading instead of going to law school or whatever. I think that except for dyslexia and that sort of thing, reading problems have more to do with people's self-images than anything else."

"I don't know," Colin said. "Maybe."

Miss Nelson tapped her pen on the table, thinking. "Colin, can you write?"

"I do my name real well," he nodded.

"I'm serious. Can you do compositions and that sort of thing?"

"I guess so. I'm not so hot with commas."

"You'll learn." She put the word lists away. "How about you meet me after school and—"

"Miss Nelson, I'm shocked!" He gasped.

"And we'll go in to see Mr. Parker," she continued. "I'm going to recommend that you be moved into Honors English."

"*Me?*"

"I think Mrs. Henderson has the class of juniors third period."

"Yeah, but—" He ran his hand through his hair. "Look, I'd rather stay here."

"Do you really think I'd let you?"

"But, I can't—" He swallowed. "I mean, I'm not—"

"I think you are. I'm sure you can handle Honors, but if you'd feel better going into a regular class . . ."

"I'd feel better staying here."

"Colin, you'll be fine. I'll help you, your new teacher will help you—" She stopped. "Which class is that girl you keep mentioning in?"

"Honors," he muttered.

"Wouldn't you feel better being in her class?"

"I don't know. Maybe."

"I think you would."

"I think I'm too stupid."

"Well, who knows," Miss Nelson said dryly. "Maybe you're right."

"What's that, reverse psychology or something?"

"I don't know, Colin. You tell me." She was very brisk now, at her desk straightening up papers. "I mean, if you're too obsequious to try, I guess that's your problem."

"Obsequious?" he asked uncertainly. "What's that got to do with it?"

Miss Nelson took off her glasses, frowning at him. "Are you kidding?" she asked.

"No." He shifted his weight to his other leg. "I mean, I don't think so."

"Do you even know what obsequious means?"

"Well, yeah." He shifted again. "At least I thought I did."

"Can you spell it?"

"I think so. O-b-s-e-q-u-i-o-u-s?"

"I see." Miss Nelson put her glasses on, very stern. "Well, can you think of a better word?"

"I don't know." He pulled on his collar with one hand, wishing he could just leave the room. "Scared? Cowardly?" He grinned slightly. "Pusillanimous?"

"I see." Miss Nelson did not look amused. "And can you spell pusillanimous?"

"Well, yeah. I think so. P-u-s-i-l-l-a-n-i—" He stopped, seeing her laughing. "What's so funny? That was right, wasn't it?"

"Exactly right," she nodded, still laughing.

"Then, what's so—" He stopped, catching on. "Oh," he said. "Guess you were kind of tricking me, huh?" He coughed, trying to keep his dignity.

"Kind of," she agreed.

"Yeah, well, just because I can spell a couple of stupid words doesn't mean—"

She cut him off. "I don't want to hear it, Mr. McNamara. I'll expect you in here right after school."

"What if I'm busy?"

"I'm sure you'll think of something."

"Maybe." He slouched over to the door, hands in his pockets. "I *am* stupid," he said defensively. "I really am."

She glanced up from her desk. "I'm sorry, Colin. Did you say something?"

"I guess not." He kept his hands in his pockets. "I kind of need a pass to get into math."

"I thought you said he'd have a heart attack if you showed up with one."

"Yeah, guess I did." He turned to leave. "Well, see ya."

She laughed, writing out a pass and handing it to him.

"Thanks." He stuffed it into his pocket. "Well, see ya."

"At two-fifteen."

"Yeah, maybe."

"Maybe definitely," she said.

"Maybe." At the door, he paused again, turning around. "Hey, Miss Nelson!"

"What?"

"Congratulations!"

"What?" She looked confused.

"On being engaged—" he gestured toward her hand. "Romance is a wonderful thing."

Right after school, he found Trish and grabbed her in a huge bear hug.

"Hi!" he said.

"Hi," she answered, startled. "What's with you?"

"Oh, I guess I'm just a bang beat, bell-ringin', big haul, great go, neck-or-nothin', rip-roarin', ever'-time-a-bull's-eye salesman."

"Wait a minute." She thought about that. "*The Music Man?*"

"Oh, kid, you're brilliant." He kissed her. "You should be in—Honors English."

"No, I should be at the drama club meeting," she remembered. "We're *finally* choosing a play. Why don't you come with me? You know more plays than anyone else in there."

He shook his head. "I don't want to. Besides, I have to go see Mr. Parker."

"What did you do?"

"You know how it is. What time you get out of your meeting?"

"I don't know, but it's in room nineteen."

"Okay, I'll wait for you." He gave her another kiss. "Later."

Trish watched him go, then turned back to her locker.

"Right out in the halls now, huh?" Mike Pilsner swaggered over.

"Oh, hi, Mike." She kept her eyes on her books. "Do we have trig homework?"

"Yeah." He moved closer. "If you want, I can come over and give you some—" he nudged her—"extra help."

"No, thanks," she said, moving away a few inches. "I think I'm all set."

"Trish Masters." He shook his head. "Who would've guessed it?"

"Oh, come on, Mike." She reached for her trig book.

"Where you wanna go?" He gave it to her.

"Cut it out, okay? It's not funny."

"Who's being funny?" His eyes roamed down. "Always figured it was a waste for someone who looks like you to be so damn pure. Tell you what," he said, flexing his arm muscles. "Come to me when you feel like trying out something bigger."

"Leave me alone, Mike." She closed her locker, hard. "It's not funny. I'm late for the drama meeting."

"We could make it so you'd be later."

She scowled and he moved back in pretended fear.

"Oooh, don't sic McNamara on me," he said. "I might have to step on him."

"He'd probably break you in half!"

"Yeah, if he could reach that high." Mike flexed his arms again. "Let me know when you change your mind."

She didn't say anything, but hurried down the hall. He caught up to her, loping easily.

"Better watch that walk," he said. "Might give people ideas."

"Look, Mike—" she spun around to face him—"I'm sick of you—"

"Hi, guys," Janet said as she, Rachael, and Peter caught up to them.

"Finally joining drama, Mike?" Peter grinned.

"No, thanks." Mike shook his head. "Trish keeps attacking me, and I was trying to get away." He glanced at his watch. "I'm late for practice; see you later."

The other three looked at Trish, who was literally shaking with anger.

"I hope the whole team tackles him," she said quietly.

"He'll break everything but his head." Rachael tried to turn it into a joke.

"Yeah, really," Peter agreed.

Very stiff, Trish walked with them.

"About time," Miss Slater, the drama coach, said as they came into Room 19. "I hope you four have some ideas— we've got it narrowed down to three plays."

"Yeah," Becky Geer, club secretary, said, glancing down at her list. "*Kiss Me, Kate, Fiddler on the Roof,* and *Oklahoma.*"

"How about *Chorus Line*?" Rachael suggested.

Miss Slater shook her head. "Don't be ridiculous. We'd never be able to handle the dancing."

"No one gets my jokes." Rachael sat down.

"I got it," Trish said. "I thought it was funny."

"Thanks," Rachael laughed. "Did you like it, Janet?"

"I've heard worse." Janet laughed too. "What'd you think, Peter?"

Miss Slater clapped her hands for silence. "Come on. This is serious business."

"I don't like any of them," one boy said.

"You don't like anything, Chuck," a girl pointed out.

"I wanted to do *Hair*." He shrugged.

"I think we should do *Eubie*," a black girl said, grinning.

"Now *there's* an idea," Rachael said.

"Think I'd make a good Tevye?" Peter asked the room in general. "I could gain fifty pounds."

Trish sat back, trying to picture Colin in the plays. Not Tevye; she couldn't see him as Tevye. And not anyone from *Kiss Me, Kate*, even though he sang the song "Brush Up Your Shakespeare" all the time. Maybe Curly In *Oklahoma;* that might be good. But there had to be something better—she snapped her fingers.

"I've got it!" she said.

"Got what?" Janet asked.

"Is it contagious?" Rachael wanted to know.

"*The Music Man!* It's perfect! Everyone loves that show."

"Hey, yeah." Peter nodded. "That'd be good."

"Can't you see the shimmer of trumpets?" Trish looked around the room. "And hear the crashing of cymbals?" She hit her hand on her desk. "Curley High needs a boys' band, and I mean, she needs it today!"

"Guess who's angling for the lead," Becky said.

"No." Trish waved that aside. "It's just such a great play! It'd be really fun. Besides, Charlestown did *Fiddler on the Roof* last year, *Oklahoma* always comes to Boston—this is perfect!"

"It might be." Janet nodded. "The costumes wouldn't be too hard."

"We could probably handle the scenery," Chuck said.

"And we could have it in my backyard!" Trish shouted.

She lowered her voice as everyone stared at her. "Sorry, got carried away."

"Trish is right," a boy said. "It would be a good play."

"Yeah, really," someone else agreed.

"Well, as long as the royalties aren't too bad, it sounds okay to me," Miss Slater said, shrugging, glad to hear people in favor of *something*. "It seems to me Newton pulled it off a couple of years ago. How many in favor of *The Music Man*?" She counted the hands. "What's the problem, Chuck?"

"I wanted to do *Hair*."

"I'll see if I can clear it through Mr. Parker tomorrow," she went on. "And if we're lucky, we can have tryouts in about two weeks. We should be able to get some scripts by then." There was a general buzz of assent, and she clapped her hands for attention. "Let's break up into committees and start making some plans."

Trish whistled a few notes under her breath as everyone noisily broke into groups.

"What did you say?" Rachael asked.

" 'With a hundred and ten cornets close at hand,' " Trish sang.

" 'They were followed by rows and rows,' " Peter joined in.

"Hey, come on." Miss Slater clapped her hands. "This is serious business."

CHAPTER FIFTEEN

"No," Colin said.

It was Sunday afternoon. They were sitting in the den of her house watching an old Fred Astaire movie, and Trish had finally gotten up the nerve to tell him about the play and ask him to try out.

"You want to hear it again?" he said. "No."

"Why not?"

He pulled his arm off her shoulders. "I don't want to."

"Oh, but the Music Man—you'd be perfect." She moved over next to him as he slid away. "Who else has enough breath control to do all those songs?"

"A lot of people." He moved away another six inches, and she followed him. "Let what's-his-name Cameron do it. Isn't he into it? There're lots of people."

"None of them are as good as you are."

"How do you know? You've never heard me."

"Yeah, I have. I've heard you sing, I've heard you quote—I know you're good." She put her arm around him. "No one has a voice as sexy as yours."

"Yeah, right." He moved her arm off. "The drama club's queer. I don't like any of those kids except for you."

"You mean, you think they don't like you."

He scowled. "How do you know what I mean?"

"Oh," she shuddered in mock fear. "We *are* defensive today."

"No, *I* am," he said. "*You're* obnoxious."

"Thanks, I like you too."

"Now, see?" He leaned forward, elbows resting on his knees. "We're in a stupid fight over this. Can't we forget about the stupid play?"

"If you want." Trish folded her arms across her chest. "You're just scared."

"I am not."

"Then why won't you do it?"

" 'Cause I don't want to; they're jerks."

Trish shrugged. "You're a jerk. I'm a jerk. We're all jerks. What can you do?"

He stared at her, then closed his eyes, shaking his head. "You're too much, Trish." He kissed her forehead. "Let's just forget about the stupid play. Promise me not to bring it up again?"

"No."

"No?"

"I can't promise. I know I'll bring it up again."

"Yeah, probably." He slung his arm around her shoulders. "Let's watch the movie."

"You're scared," she said, leaning back against his chest.

"Yeah, so what?" he asked. "Hey, did I tell you?"

"What?"

"They're moving me into a regular English class tomorrow."

"No, you didn't tell me." She pulled away. "Colin, that's great!"

He shrugged. "Might be okay."

"You'll be wonderful—straight A's!"

"That'll be the day." He swallowed, his hands clasping together. "Think the people in the class'll hate me?"

She grinned. "Because you're so smart?" Her smile faded as she saw that he was serious. "No, of course not."

"They'll think I'm a jerk; they already do."

"Well, you're not." She covered his hand with hers. "You'll be fine."

"I'm kind of scared to death," he gulped.

"You'll be fine."

He shook his head. "I don't think I can do it. I should have told Parker I didn't want to switch. God, Trish, I don't want to switch." He moved closer so she would put her arm around him. "You think they'll hate me?"

"Not when they find out how wonderful you are."

"No, I'm serious. Are they gonna hate me?"

"No." Her voice was very sure.

"If they do," he said weakly, "I'm holding you responsible."

"I take full responsibility." She kissed his cheek. "Don't be scared; it'll be okay."

"Yeah, right." He rested his head against hers. "Let's just watch the movie."

Trish sat in English class the next morning, talking with Janet, Rachael, Peter, and Chuck about the play. She hadn't mentioned that Colin might try out. She wasn't planning on mentioning it either. They kept talking, waiting for their teacher, Mrs. Henderson, to start class. The door opened, and Mr. Parker came in. He and Mrs. Henderson talked for a minute, then she looked at the door.

"Well, where is he?" she asked.

"What?" Mr. Parker turned around, realizing that he hadn't been followed in, and went back to the door. "Uh, Colin?"

Every head in the room snapped up as Colin came in, wearing jeans and a work shirt with the sleeves rolled up, looking at no one, but at everyone, a six-hundred-pound chip on his shoulder.

"Do you all know Colin McNamara?" Mr. Parker asked. "He'll be in your class from now on."

"But can he *read*?" Mike Pilsner muttered from the back of the room.

"Do you want something, Mr. Pilsner?" Mrs. Henderson asked.

Mike shrugged. "I didn't say anything."

"Thank you very much," Mrs. Henderson said to Mr. Parker. "I think we're all set."

The principal nodded, gave Colin a clap on the shoulder, and left the room.

"Well, Colin," Mrs. Henderson said, handing him a book, "sit down."

Colin scanned the room, saw an empty seat, and headed for it.

"McNamara in *here?*" someone asked. "Talk about mainstreaming."

"Mr. Freedman—" Mrs. Henderson started.

"I'll handle it," Colin said abruptly, glancing at the room in general. "Look," he growled, both fists coming together. "Anyone has anything to say, they can say it to me after."

The room was quiet. Then, unexpectedly, Rachael spoke up.

"I'm glad you're here," she said, looking at Mike Pilsner and Sam Freedman. "We need some nice guys."

A grin jerked at Colin's mouth.

"Thanks," he said, sitting down. "I'll pay you after class." He threw his book open and leaned back to wait for class to begin.

Trish looked at Rachael, very impressed. Then she reached her hand across the aisle, and she and Rachael shook.

"Speaking of nice people . . ." Trish said.

As soon as class was over, she crossed to his desk, getting there before he even had time to stand up.

"Why didn't you tell me it was *this* English class?" she asked.

"I forgot."

"And I sat there telling you 'good luck' like an idiot."

He patted her on the head, then noticed Rachael moving past.

"Hey!" he called.

"What?" She turned halfway.

"Thank you."

Rachael shrugged, embarrassed, and kept going.

Trish put her arm on his shoulder. "Hey, Mac . . ."

"The name's Colin, kid."

"We've got lunch now. Will you sit with me?"

He glanced around the emptying room.

"Do this twice in one day?" He shuddered.

"Please?"

"Can he resist a beautiful girl?" Colin asked his book. He looked up. "Pilsner sit at your table?"

"Yeah." Trish scowled. "*He's* the one who shouldn't be in the class. I swear they only did it so he can get a stupid sports scholarship."

"I'm gonna break the guy's face in half."

"Come on, I just want to sit there and have you hold my hand."

"An offer he cannot refuse," Colin told his book. He reached down and took her hand. "Let's go already."

As they sat down at the table in the cafeteria, she could feel his hand trembling and gave it a squeeze. He sat very stiffly, not opening his lunch bag.

"You aren't going to eat?" she whispered.

"I'm not hungry."

"You don't have to sit here if you won't want to."

He glanced at the table of people all carefully ignoring him.

"But I do." His voice was stilted. "Look how much fun I'm having. See Colin enjoying himself."

"You'd better stop," Trish said, holding his hand very tightly. "Because if you don't, I'm going to have to give you this wild, passionate kiss and everyone'll look at us."

He grinned. "Might be worth it."

"Well, yeah, it's a good play," one of the girls was saying to Janet, who was sitting across from them. "But there's no one around here who can play the lead. None of them can act *and* sing."

"Some of them might have gotten better since last year," Janet pointed out.

"Maybe," the girl said.

Trish squeezed Colin's hand, her expression innocent.

"Never give up, do you?" he muttered.

"Never." She gave him half of her sandwich. "Here, Mom made turkey."

He accepted it, taking a shy, one-handed bite, avoiding everyone's eyes.

Mike Pilsner, coming back from the cafeteria line with two ice-cream sandwiches and an open carton of milk, paused.

"Will ya look at the riff-raff they're letting in?" he said in an extra-loud voice.

Trish, holding Colin's hand, felt him stiffen.

"I'm gonna break him in half," Colin growled.

Trish kept her grip on his hand. "No, you're not."

"Why don't you get out of here, McNamara?" Mike said, wandering down to their end of the table, still holding the carton of milk. "No one wants you."

Trish kept her hand tight, feeling the suppressed, trembling fury in Colin.

"Yeah, hold the little boy's hand," Mike sneered. "I'm surprised that's all you're doing to him. Why don't you *both* go sit with scum?"

Colin started to jump up, but Trish beat him to it, making sure that her shoulder hit the bottom of Mike's milk carton on the way. The milk splashed out, drenching him.

"Will you watch where you're going, Mike?" she demanded.

"You little—" He stopped his hand from drawing back, as he spotted a teacher hurrying over.

"What's the problem?" the teacher asked.

"No problem," Mike said through gritted teeth, wiping his face with one sleeve. "Guess I just spilled my milk."

"Well, why don't you go out to the Boys' Room and get cleaned up," the teacher suggested firmly.

"Yeah." Mike shot Trish a venomous look, then headed for the door.

She let out her breath, swallowing her fear.

"He was going to—" Colin's voice shook.

"Everything's okay." She gripped his hand, giving the entire table a challenging look. No one said anything. She sat down and started to eat again.

Slowly, uneasily, everyone else at the table followed suit, exchanging glances, then returning to interrupted conversations.

"Okay," Colin said.

She looked over at him. "What?"

"I'll try out."

"You will?"

"Yeah," he said. "You did that for me, I'll do this for you."

"What about the reading?"

"Did that for *me*." He started to pick up his sandwich, but saw the clumsy ball of bread and turkey. "Sorry, guess I squeezed the sandwich."

"That's okay." She handed him her half.

"You're not hungry?"

She shook her head. He started to pick it up, then set it back down.

"Neither am I," he said.

There was another drama-club meeting after school, with a poster-making session scheduled for afterward. Trish, Rachael, and Janet found themselves alone in the room when the meeting was over. They had collected felt-tipped markers from various teachers, and the art department had contributed a pile of posterboard.

"Did you ever notice we end up making a lot of posters?" Rachael asked wryly.

"We make good ones," Trish said.

"No," Janet corrected her. "We're just chumps who let ourselves get talked into things."

"How come Peter didn't stay?" Rachael had selected a piece of posterboard; now she sat down on the floor with it, sketching out what she was going to write.

"He *said* he had a dentist appointment." Janet tried to read what Rachael had written. "What are we supposed to put on these, anyway?"

" 'Play tryouts. Thursday, 2:30–5:00. Singers, dancers, actors.' " Trish said, quoting the little list Miss Slater had left them.

"Catchy," Rachael nodded, uncapping a Magic Marker and starting to write. "God, I hate how these stupid things squeak."

Janet started lettering. "I hate how these stupid things smell."

"I hate how they taste," Trish said.

Janet and Rachael looked at her.

Trish shrugged. "I felt left out."

"Oh, no." Janet put her marker down. "I ran out of room."

" 'PLAY TRYOU—' " Rachael read aloud.

"Can I put the 'TS' on the next line without it looking stupid?"

The other two shook their heads. Janet sighed, and flipped the cardboard over to start again.

Rachael held up her poster. "How's this?"

" 'Wanted: A Music Man with *Soul*,' " Janet read.

"We've got to get you white kids out of this." Instead Rachael drew an African Music Man.

"I think Music *Man* is sexist," Janet decided. "How about we call it, *The Music Person*?"

"I'm trapped in a room with maniacs," Trish said to no one in particular.

"You think Peter'll end up getting it?" Rachael asked. "There's not really anyone else."

"He can't sing," Janet said. "I mean, not well."

"Todd Roberts can." Rachael gave her funky African some green beads. "Only he can't act."

"The show'll be lousy if the lead isn't good." Janet ran out of room before she finished "PLAY TRYOUTS" again, and reached for a fresh piece of posterboard. "Becky'll get

Marian, and she'll be good. But, the Music Man," she shook her head. "Why'd you suggest such a stupid show, Trish?"

"Why'd you vote for it?" Trish highlighted her big red "PLAY TRYOUTS" with blue and green.

"You ask me," Rachael commented, "she really railroaded it through."

Trish kept highlighting. "Yup."

"*She* wants to be the lead." Janet started highlighting, liking the effect on Trish's poster.

"Hey, wait a minute." Rachael stopped in the middle of writing the word "Thursday." "I think it's a plot. I think she has someone in mind for the lead."

"I think you've been inhaling Magic Markers," Trish said.

"You were pretty enthusiastic," Janet said.

"You know," Rachael pulled Trish's poster over and started drawing an African on it. "There's only one guy you'd go to so much trouble for."

There was a hesitant knock on the door, and Colin peeked in.

"Uh, hi," he said. "You 'bout done, Trish?"

She shook her head. "We just started. Want to help?"

"What're you doing?" He put his hands in his pockets.

"Posters," Rachael said, holding up one.

"*Music Man*, huh?" He sat down on a desk. "That a good show?"

"It's very good," Trish said.

"Boy, though," Rachael said, starting a new poster. "We'll never find anyone to play the lead. No one around here's good enough."

"Yeah," Janet agreed. "Miss Slater has this fantasy that some gifted person's going to show up the day of tryouts."

Colin shrugged, sitting down next to Trish and watching her write. "Maybe Robert Preston'll come," he said.

"Are you sure he was in it?" Janet asked doubtfully.

"Well, yeah," Colin said. "God, he was—" He stopped, catching on. "I mean, so you hear."

Trish rescued him. "Want to do a poster, Mac?"

"I write messy."

"Do a poster." She gave him some cardboard and a green Magic Marker. He sighed and studied her poster to see what to write.

"Boy, though," Rachael's voice was elaborately casual. "Sure would be great if some person would come from nowhere and be able to play the lead. Yeah, sure would be great. I mean, Trish, you were so big on doing the show, and we don't even have anyone to play the lead."

Colin scowled at Trish, who smiled weakly.

"Boy, that sure would be good," she said.

"Sure would." Janet nodded.

"You said it," Rachael agreed.

Colin looked at the three of them industriously making their posters and scowled harder, bending over his.

CHAPTER SIXTEEN

"I changed my mind," he said as the two of them walked down the hall after school Thursday. "I'm not trying out."

"Then how come you're walking down toward the auditorium?" Trish wanted to know.

"Keeping you company."

"Right." She peeked through the window in the auditorium door and saw that tryouts had already started. A boy was just leaving the stage, and Peter was going up for his turn.

"We shouldn't have been late," Colin said. "Let's just not go in. Your friends said they wouldn't tell anyone I was thinking of maybe doing it."

"We're only a little late." Trish pulled the door open. "There's not that many people trying out for the lead."

"Then I'll skip it." He put shaking hands into his pockets. "That'll give them a better chance."

"Come on, you promised."

"How about I buy you flowers?" he whispered, following her in. "You like flowers?"

"No, I hate them." She sat down in the back of the darkened auditorium.

"You do?" He sat next to her, still whispering. "How can you hate flowers? No one hates flowers."

"Look." She put her hand on his arm. "I'm the assistant stage manager, I really have to go up there. I told her I was only going to be a few minutes late. You're going to be terrific."

"I'm going to be lousy." He twisted in his seat, watching the stage. "Oh, God."

"What's wrong?"

"He's good."

"You're much better."

"I am not."

"He can't sing."

"They said Rex Harrison couldn't either." He stiffened as Miss Slater smiled and murmured, "Good job, Peter," and another boy climbed up to the stage to try out. "Who's this guy? Looks pretty queer."

"He can really sing."

"Oh, God." Colin slumped down. "Look, no one's seen me—maybe I should just go."

"You're going to be great."

"I want to forget it, I really do." He stood up. "I'll be an arsonist when I grow up."

"Come on." She yanked him back down. "You're going to be great. I really have to get up there, so break a leg. And don't forget to fill out your form."

"What form? What are you getting me into?" He started slumping again. "God, this is awful. Think I'll be a truck driver."

"No, you won't." She kissed him swiftly. "Break a leg."

"Will you speak to me again if I screw up?"

"If you give it your best."

"Yeah, well, see ya." He slumped into his shirt collar. "Been nice knowing you."

"I promise I'll cheer." She kissed him again and hurried up to the front of the auditorium. "Hi," she whispered to Miss Slater. "Sorry I'm late."

"No problem." Miss Slater, the director, gave her a clipboard. "Start taking down people's names and what roles they're trying out for. And ask Martha if she needs any help."

Trish nodded and went over to Martha, the stage manager.

Tryouts continued smoothly, if a little blandly, a few more people trying out for the lead. When she finally reached the end of the pile of audition forms, Miss Slater looked up.

"Anyone else trying out for the Professor?" she asked.

No one moved.

"Okay then." She glanced down. "Why don't we have—"

Colin stood up, shoved his hands into his pockets, and slouched down the aisle.

"Uh," he coughed. "Guess I kind of didn't try out yet, sorry."

"Oh." Miss Slater looked very surprised. Then she recovered herself. "For the lead? Did you fill out your form?"

"What stupid form?" He shot a glance at Trish.

"Just this." She handed him a mimeographed sheet.

His hands shook as he reached out to get it and he withdrew, embarrassed.

"What is it?" His hands went back into his pockets.

"Well, you write down your experience and—"

"I don't have any."

"Oh. Well." She blinked twice. "Why don't you not worry about your form for now." She picked up a script, opening to one of the audition scenes. "Do you, um, want to read this?"

"I *can* read," he said stiffly.

"I know." She nodded. "Do you know the story? Basically, it's about—"

"I've seen it."

"Oh." She blinked again. "Okay, then, would you like to read?"

"Guess so." He looked at Trish reproachfully.

"Why don't you go up then? Becky," she said, turning, "how about you read the scene starting on page sixty with him?"

"Sure." Becky stood up, tall, blond, and the obvious choice for the female lead.

"Do you sing, Colin?" Miss Slater asked.

141

"No, not really." He slouched up after Becky, sensing her masked amusement at reading with him. It was almost as if she were a stodgy old relative humoring a young and not very intelligent nephew. Colin's hands tightened around the script and he gulped down sudden waves of fear. He'd never felt stage fright when he practiced in his room.

"Ready to go?" Becky asked.

"Guess so."

She waited for him to begin.

"Well?" she asked after a minute.

"Aren't you going to walk in?"

"Oh. Through the door, you mean?" She spoke with an edge of sarcasm.

"You're supposed to be an actress. Can't you fake it?"

"Well—"

"We're only reading today," Miss Slater cut in. "Just start, don't worry about it."

"Oh." He frowned down at the script, a thick knot of tension replacing his vocal cords. "Well, I—" His free hand fluttered into his pocket. "I—" He wiped his other arm across his face, perspiring.

"You can start," Miss Slater said.

"Uh, yeah." He swallowed, then looked at Becky. "Can I ask you something?"

"Sure."

"Are you, like, just humoring me?" His sleeve went back across his face.

"No. Everyone's allowed to try out."

"Even me, huh?" He ruffled up his hair with one hand. "I'm not trying out to be a jerk or anything; I'm really not."

"I know." Becky hadn't, but she believed him. "Loosen up, you know?"

"I'm trying."

"Would you feel better singing first?" Miss Slater asked, glancing at her watch.

"Guess so. What do I sing?"

"Whatever you want," Miss Slater said. "Preferably something from the show."

"Yeah." He scowled at Trish. "How about 'The Sadder But Wiser Girl'?"

Miss Slater nodded. "Okay. Mrs. Ching can—"

"I don't need a pianist." Suddenly all business, he turned his back, putting the script down and taking several deep breaths, wishing that Ophelia were the only one in the audience. He squared his shoulders and spun around, looking oddly taller, putting a confident, conspiring arm around Becky. As he started singing, almost everyone in the auditorium straightened up. The formerly arrogant half-grin was now wry self-amusement, and people began laughing in the right places as he used Becky for a prop, as people he'd be singing to.

" 'I smile, I grin, when the gal with a touch of sin walks in, I hope and I pray—' " Now he was on his knees. " 'For Hester to win just *one* more A, the sadder but wiser girl's the girl for me, the sadder but wiser girl for me!' " As he finished, lying in a mock dip next to Becky, a low, approving murmur ran through the people watching.

"You're really good," Becky said. "You know that?"

He grinned and scrambled to his feet, not even out of breath.

"Well," Miss Slater said, stunned. "Can you—can you do the first part of 'Ya Got Trouble'?"

He shrugged. "Guess so." He took a deep breath and started a brisk, pushing rhythm. Unsure when Miss Slater was going to stop him, Colin kept going. Looking out, he could see everyone enjoying the song, and he warmed to the rhythm, hammering it along.

He was a good way through when Miss Slater snapped out of her trance.

"Oh, good, very good," she said finally. "You want to try a monologue? We've got a few from dramatic shows here."

He shrugged. "Yeah, I guess."

She lifted several paperbacks, hands almost trembling with the fear that this talented apparition might not be real. "Do you have a preference?"

"Uh," he squinted at the titles. "How about that 'Long Journey' thing?"

"*Long Day's Journey into Night?*"

He nodded. "Yeah, that's the one."

"Okay." She handed him up the script. "There's a passage on page one fifty-three by Edmund, the son."

Colin flipped to the page.

"Edmund's looking back in this scene," she went on. "And—"

"Can I do a different one?" he interrupted.

"A different one?" She stopped. "Oh. Well, I guess so. Did you have something in mind?"

"Yeah." He moved back a few pages. "This one, on one forty-nine." He looked out at the people watching. "This is the father, James, kind of a failure. He and his son are a little crocked and he's talking about the old days, about being an actor, and pretty much how he blew his life." He frowned. "You got a chair or something?"

Miss Slater pointed and he dragged a chair and a rickety desk out to the front of the stage.

"This is the table, we're playing cards," he explained, sitting down. He flashed a grin at the audience in general, but mostly at Trish. "Casino," he said.

Colin ran up his front stoop and inside, whistling the first few bars of "Seventy-Six Trombones." He heard his mother in the kitchen and rushed in, giving her a huge hug and a kiss on the cheek.

"Well, hi," she said, forgetting that she had the phone in one hand. "What was that for?"

"Because I love you." He hugged her again.

"Harriet, I'll call you back," she said into the phone, then hung up.

Mr. McNamara came in, just home from work, obviously

tired and depressed, his uniform shirt unbuttoned. Colin moved over and hugged him.

"Hi, Dad," he said, hugging harder. "I love you."

Mr. McNamara stared at his son, confused. Seeing Ophelia wandering in, Colin released his father and picked her up, hugging her.

"Hi, cat." He buried his head in her fur. "I love you too."

Mr. McNamara went over to one of the cabinets and took out a bottle of Scotch.

"What are you doing?" Colin asked.

"If y've flipped out, lad, I'm going to be needing it." He took out a glass.

"But I'm fine. I'm great!" Colin did a quick soft-shoe.

"What happened?" his mother asked.

"Lots and lots!" Colin started to sit down, but jumped up. "Like, I haven't told you guys anything! I know, we'll go out to dinner!" He studied his parents. "No, you look tired. I'll bring dinner here! How about pizza? You like pizza? Like, with pepperoni and junk?" He gave his father a gentle punch in the stomach. "Wear a tie, it's good news!" He grabbed his jacket and headed for the door.

"D'ye need some money, lad?" his father called after him.

"Oh, yeah, money!" Colin raced back.

"Is fifteen enough?" His father gave him two bills.

"It's wonderful!" Colin hugged him. "You're wonderful! Everything's wonderful! Back right away!" He ran out of the house, singing "Seventy-Six Trombones."

Mr. McNamara poured himself a drink.

"I think he's flipped out, Maureen," he said.

She shrugged. "Well, I hope he stays this way."

CHAPTER SEVENTEEN

Janet shook her head. "I've never seen anyone as happy as that kid in my life," she said as she and Trish walked down the hall a few days later.

"You haven't seen his parents." Trish grinned. "I was over there this weekend and it was like neither of them ever sat down."

"Half the girls around here are jealous of you."

"Good." Trish's grin widened. "Did Peter ask you to Chuck's party yet?"

"Yeah. You two going?"

"I think so," Trish said. "Colin's kind of nervous about it."

"Well, you've got almost two weeks to work on him."

"Yeah," Trish agreed. "All we have to do now is get Rachael fixed up."

"She still likes Mr. Caprio."

"I sure do," Rachael said, catching up with them. "What a body that guy has."

"I bet he can pick up a bus," Janet said.

"I like my men big—"

"Uh, look," Trish said, stopping suddenly. "How about I meet you guys there?"

Janet stopped too. "What's wrong?"

"Nothing." Trish shook her head too hard. "I just left something in my locker."

"No, you didn't." Rachael noticed Mike Pilsner farther up the hall with some of his friends from the football team. "Is he still bugging you?"

"Yeah," Trish said briefly, books clutched to her chest. "It doesn't matter, I'll just—"

146

Two of the boys left the group and walked past them, staring pointedly at Trish. One nudged the other and they both laughed.

"Ignore them," Rachael said. "They're all jerks."

"Yeah." Trish smiled tightly.

"Come on," Janet said. "We'll just walk right by them. It's not like you're alone."

"I don't want to."

"You want him to know he's getting to you?" Rachael asked.

"I don't care." Trish shifted her weight to her other leg, starting to get panicky. "Look, I'll just go the other way." She hurried down the hall, her two friends following.

Janet caught up first. "You know what? You should tell Colin."

Trish shook her head. "Uh-uh. He's so happy right now, I don't want to ruin it. Besides, it doesn't matter."

"Then how come you look like you're about to cry?" Rachael wanted to know.

"I'm tired." Trish clutched her books, keeping the tears back.

Mike and his other two friends came up behind them, Mike managing to bump into her, hard enough to knock her books out of her arms.

"Jesus." He kicked the trig book. "Will you watch where you're going?"

"Why don't you?" Rachael demanded.

Trish didn't say anything, but bent to pick up her books.

Janet put her hands on her hips. "Yeah, you're really a jerk. Why don't you just cut it out, Mike?"

He grinned. "You two better watch yourselves. Hanging around her, you're gonna get lousy reputations."

"You two better watch *yourselves*." Rachael looked at his two friends, hulking seniors. "Hanging around him, you'll get reputations as stegosaurus brains."

"Oooh." Both boys backed away, laughing.

"Hard core," one said. "I'm scared now."

"See you later, Mike," the other said. "Ya said ya wanted to get in a quick one, right?"

"Yeah." He nodded. "Looks like I'm in the right place." He gave Trish a light punch on the arm. "I'll be over at the usual time."

She flinched away, eyes on her books. He laughed, running after his friends.

"God." Rachael stared after him. "He's not kidding, is he?"

"Don't let him bother you," Janet advised. "He's not worth it."

"I'm not bothered." Trish gulped, not looking up. "We'd better get going."

They all started down the hall again.

"He can't keep doing that," Rachael scowled. "We have to—"

"Hey." Trish looked up, under control now, despite the tears brimming in her eyes. "You've got to promise you won't tell Colin, or have anyone tell him. If you do, I swear I'll never speak to you again."

Janet and Rachael exchanged glances.

"You'd probably speak to us again," Janet said finally.

"No, I wouldn't." Trish ran a trembling hand through her hair. "Just let him be happy; he needs it. Don't worry, I can handle this."

"By yourself?" Rachael asked.

"Yeah. It's not that big a deal."

"So how come you're crying?" Janet wanted to know.

"I'm not." Trish suddenly felt moisture on her face and closed her eyes. "I'll meet you guys at rehearsal." She started down the hall, walking fast, almost running.

"Trish . . ." Rachael began.

"I left something in my locker, okay?" Trish walked even faster.

After rehearsal ended that afternoon, Trish stayed in her seat, staring up at the stage, until most people had left.

Peter, who had gotten the role of the Music Man's sidekick, came over and sat next to her. "What are you doing?" he asked.

"Thinking about how hard the sets are going to be." She shook her head. "Ten times worse than last year."

"Hey, you're the one who wanted to do this show." He smiled. "Where's Colin?"

"He had to get home. How are we going to manage the town?"

"Backdrops?"

"I guess." She studied her clipboard. "I've got a bunch of stupid little things to do. You don't have to hang around if you don't want to."

"I'll give you a hand." He followed her up on stage. "What exactly does assistant stage manager mean?"

"That I'm afraid of full responsibility." Trish moved the two chairs by the curtain off stage right.

"And that you get stuck with the dirty work."

"That, too." Trish grinned. "I feel like all I do is go down to the clinic to get Miss Slater aspirin."

"You should have tried out. You would have made it."

"I'd be too scared," she said. "You guys can do the acting; I'd rather hide backstage."

"You know, Colin's really good." He pulled the curtain for her. "I mean, like—wow. Professional good."

"I know." She dragged a table into the back space. "I couldn't believe it the first time I saw him. You should hear him do Shakespeare."

"The guy reads Shakespeare too?"

"All the time."

"Wow." Peter sat down on the risers the high-school choir stored backstage. "He sure managed to make everyone think he was stupid."

"Well, he's a good actor." Trish sat on the risers too.

"I can't get the guy to talk, though. The minute you leave the room, he just shuts up and waits for you to come back.

149

He'll talk about the scenes we have to do together, but that's about it."

"He's shy." Trish played with her right shoelace. "He thinks no one likes him."

"It's just jerks like Pilsner and that crowd."

"Yeah." Trish tied the boat moccasin very tightly.

"Mike's giving you a pretty rough time, isn't he?"

"Did Janet tell you to talk to me?" she asked suddenly.

"She didn't have to. He's being pretty lousy, isn't he?"

"A little. I think he's still mad about the milk."

"He was really bugged about that," Peter agreed. "Half of it is just that he's jealous of Colin. He really likes you."

"Funny, I didn't get that feeling."

"He's like that." Peter leaned back on his elbows. "He doesn't know how to handle girls, just gets drunk and tries to attack them—well, you know that."

"Yeah." She moved to her left shoelace. "Has he been saying things about me? I mean, like, around boys."

"I don't know." Peter shrugged into his collar.

"You do too. Has he been saying stuff in the locker room and places like that?"

"Kind of," he admitted.

"Like what?"

"I don't know, stuff."

"Well, like what?" she asked uneasily.

"Trish, come on."

"You come on. What's he been saying?"

"A lot of junk. It's mostly just talk."

"What kind of talk?"

"The same old stuff about you sleeping around." Peter pulled his collar up. "Everyone knows it isn't true. Then he says stuff about you leading him on, and the way you walk—you know."

"What's wrong with the way I walk?" Trish asked stiffly.

"Nothing."

150

"Then how come he talks about it?"

"It's sexy," Peter said. "It's not your fault."

"But I don't do anything," she said, turning red.

"You're cute, don't knock it." He blushed too. "Guys always talk about the way people walk—even before you started seeing Colin."

"I don't do anything on purpose," she said. "I really don't. I just walk."

"That's probably why it's sexy." He turned even redder than she was, and sank lower, practically pulling his collar over his head. "Now you're going to think I'm perverted. It's not that I look or anything, it's just—don't get hung up about it. I didn't mean to say anything." Looking at her, he had to smile. "You're so cute. I don't know how Mike could be so mean to you."

"Well, what do I do?"

"I don't know, I've been trying to talk to him, and I know Chuck did too. The only thing you can really do is try to ignore him. If he knows he's getting to you, he'll keep it up."

"I guess so." She sighed.

"Don't worry, he'll give up after a while." He leaned over to read the list of things to do on her clipboard. "Want me to give you a hand with the lights?"

CHAPTER EIGHTEEN

Over the next few days, Trish did her best to ignore Mike and his friends. But when no one else was around, he seemed to be worse than ever. She was so jumpy, she expected to hear a leering male voice every time she stepped out into the hall.

"Hey, what's with you?" Colin demanded as they left rehearsal on Wednesday afternoon.

"What do you mean?" she said, pulling on her ski jacket.

"All I do is put my stupid hand on your shoulder and you jump about thirty feet. I sit down, you stand up—you're driving me crazy! What did I do?"

"Nothing." She zipped up her jacket. "You're paranoid."

"Yeah, get your armor on," he said, scowling at the jacket. "You've got to be protected: I might touch you or something."

She shrugged defensively. "It's cold."

"Yeah, well, couldn't I have put my arm around you? What is it, do you think I'm gross?"

"You know I don't."

"So what's the problem?"

"Nothing." She started stiffly down the hall.

"Trish, come on." He moved after her. "Why won't you talk to me? Why won't you tell me what's wrong?"

"Because nothing's wrong."

He frowned. "Hey, did you hurt your leg or something? You've been walking funny lately."

She flushed.

"I've been walking the way I always do," she said.

"Lately you walk like you're in a body cast."

"Thanks a lot." Trish zipped her jacket up even higher.

"What, are you mad because I have to kiss Becky in that scene?"

"No." Trish considered that for a minute. "Well, now that I think about it, it bugs me, but that's not it."

"So what is?"

"I told you, I'm tired."

"You didn't tell me."

"Oh. Well, I told someone," she said, rubbing her forehead; a terrible headache was starting to pound.

"Well, all I know is you're mad." He sulkily untucked his shirt. "Is it me? Do you not like me anymore?"

"You know that isn't it." She touched his arm. "I'm sorry, I've been in a bad mood for a few days."

"Oh, I know." He nodded. "It's okay, I understand."

"You do?" She was confused by his knowing tone.

"Hormones and junk. Sorry, I forgot."

"Oh, Colin," she laughed, giving him a brief hug. "That was two weeks ago. And I was a joy to be around."

"You were," he remembered. Then he frowned. "So what's your excuse?"

"I'm tired."

"I would have said Grumpy." He zipped and unzipped her jacket, thinking. "Okay, okay, I've got it. I've got a wonderful idea."

"What?"

"Here." He handed her a dime.

"What's this for?"

"Go call your mother. My father's at work, my mother had to go to some christening—you can come to my apartment and I'll make you dinner. Don't worry, you'll be home early."

"You'll make dinner?" Trish asked dubiously. "Can you cook?"

"Julia Child comes to *my* class," he said. "Go call your mother and I'll get my books and everything and meet you back here."

"Okay." Trish started to smile. "Sounds good." She headed down the hall, then paused. "Hey, wait."

"What?"

"Are you going to get me drunk and seduce me?"

"If you want."

"Think I'll just go call my mother." She hurried down toward the corridor by the gymnasium, figuring that it would be the only unlocked part of the building that had a phone. She took a right, walking faster.

"Shake it, don't break it!" a voice called.

She stiffened, seeing one of Mike's friends coming out of the boys' locker room after wrestling practice. The football players were now doing their winter sports. She turned to the phone, swiftly dialing, as the boy smirked his way past.

"Hi, Mom?" she said when her mother answered. "Is it okay if I have dinner at Colin's house? I'll be home early."

"Is it all right with his mother?" Mrs. Masters asked.

"Oh, no problem," Trish said, knowing that Mrs. McNamara wouldn't mind.

"Well, okay. You're missing pork chops. Be home by eight-thirty, okay?"

"Okay, thanks." Trish hung up, turning to see Mike right behind her, leaning up against the wall.

"Going my way?" he asked.

"Excuse me." She tried to get past him, walking swiftly, reminding herself that she was going to ignore him.

"What's wrong?" He had noticed the walk. "You doing too much wrestling too?"

She hunched her shoulders and, feeling very exposed, kept going.

Colin jogged down to meet her. "Did she say it was okay?"

"Yeah."

"What's wrong? You—" He saw Mike leaving through the far door. "Hey, he wasn't bugging you, was he?"

She shook her head.

"You sure? I'll break his face in half if he was." Colin's fists were already coming together.

"He wasn't," she said. "Come on, let's go."

"Well, you let me know if he does."

She nodded.

When they were at Colin's apartment, he sat her down in the living room, giving her a glass of Tab with three ice cubes.

"Okay," he said. "I'll get things going in there. I'll bring you out some dip in a minute."

"I can't help you?"

"*No one* helps the Great McNamara."

Trish laughed, leaning back on the couch as he left the room. She saw the paper on the coffee table and picked it up, starting to read the front page. Colin came back in after a few minutes, holding a tray with a small parsley-garnished dish, three different kinds of crackers, and some chunks of cheddar cheese.

"Here." He fixed her a cracker with dip, handed it to her on a napkin, and folded his arms across his chest to watch her eat it. "What do you think?"

"It's good," she nodded, impressed. "What's in it?"

"The Great McNamara never reveals his secrets." He grinned, and fixed one for himself. "It's got curry and junk; I made it up. Here—" He handed her another. "I've got to go back in there. Do you like mushrooms?"

"Yeah, sure. But, can't I help you? I could make a salad."

"I guess you could do that," he agreed. "But that's all."

She laughed. "I'll do my best not to offend the Great McNamara."

In the kitchen, he got out two aprons, keeping the one with thick blue-and-white stripes, giving her a smaller, calico one.

"You can get a bowl from that cupboard," he said, pointing. "Remember: tear the lettuce, don't cut it."

"Why not?"

"The knife makes it taste metallic." He took out lettuce, a large tomato, two carrots, half a green pepper, and a Bermuda onion. "You like radishes?"

"Sure."

He pulled out what was left of a bagful of radishes, as well as a cucumber and some celery.

"There." He studied the pile. "You all set?"

"Do you have Parmesan cheese?"

"I guess so, why?"

"Masterful Masters always puts two spoonfuls on her salad." She grinned. "It gives the vegetables that special tang."

"Yeah?" He took out the jar. "Well, go to it, woman." He leaned inside the refrigerator. "How about hamburgers with the onion-soup mix—and like mushrooms and cheese and all, stuffed potatoes, and maybe some green beans?"

"Wonderful." She made the salad, listening to him bustle around behind her, thoroughly enjoying himself. When she had finished, she put the salad bowl and the leftover vegetables in the refrigerator. "Do you like Russian dressing?"

"If it's good." He stirred the mushrooms and onions which were quietly frying over low heat.

"I served it to the Queen last time she was over."

"Go to it, woman."

Finished before he was, Trish sat down at the table to watch him work; with his sleeves rolled up, and concentrating intently, he looked very serious, and very handsome.

"You know what?" she asked suddenly.

He crossed two half strips of bacon over each of the hamburgers, then covered them with foil until it was time to cook them. "What?"

"You're *really* sexy."

"Yeah?" He looked very pleased.

"Wow."

He stood a little taller, untying his apron, fixing himself a glass of Coke.

"Come on," he said, taking her hand. "The hamburgers don't go in for twenty minutes—I'll make a fire."

"How romantic."

"I was hoping you'd think so."

She sat on the couch, helping herself to more dip.

He pointed. "Can you toss me those matches?"

She flipped him the package and he lit the fire, which blazed up perfectly.

"The Great McNamara strikes again." He came over and sat next to her. "You don't have to eat it to be polite."

"It's great." She fixed herself another cracker.

"Good."

They sat in silence for a few pleasant moments, watching the fire burn down to a steady, even flame, listening to the wood crackle.

"Could I ask you something?" she said, moving closer.

He put his arm around her. "Yeah, sure."

"Can I kiss you?"

"Wow." He put his glass down, the glow from the fire moving to his eyes.

"My father says it's good manners to ask."

"Wow." He put his other arm around her. "That's like, the sexiest thing I ever heard."

She grinned. "I was hoping you'd think so."

After a quiet dinner, they washed the dishes together, still not saying much, just enjoying being with each other.

"When you have to be home?" he said as he hung up the damp dish towels.

"Mom said eight-thirty. When're your parents coming home?"

"Mom said nine-thirty."

They both nodded, somewhat awkward.

"You really are a good cook," she said.

"Thanks. Sometimes I get into it."

They both nodded.

"Would you mind if I used your bathroom?" she asked.

"What? Oh, no. Come on, you know where it is?" They

went down the hall and he pointed. "In there. I'm pretty sure there're clean towels and everything."

When she came out, he was nowhere in sight. His bedroom door was slightly ajar, and she peeked inside and saw him leaning up against his desk with his script.

"There you are," she said.

"Gotta keep practicing."

"No one can believe how good you are," she said, coming all the way into the room.

"Am I really doing okay?"

"Looking for praise, huh?" She gravitated toward his bookcase.

He put his script down and crossed over behind her, putting his arms around her waist.

"Hey," he said.

"Hey, what?" She tilted her head to see him.

"Can I kiss you?"

She twisted to face him, arms going around his neck.

"Can I take that as a yes?" He leaned against his shelves, pulling her close, and they embraced for a long minute. "Hey," he murmured. "Wanna move over there?"

She stiffened. "Where?"

"The bed, where you think?"

"No." She shook her head strenuously. "No, I don't want to."

"We're not gonna *do* anything. It'd just be more comfortable."

"Well . . ." Trish hesitated. "What if your mother came home?"

He reached out with one hand, shutting the door.

"She'll knock." He sat down on the edge of the bed. "Come on."

"I don't know," she said, keeping her distance.

"Come on."

Uneasily, she sat next to him.

"Now was that so bad?" He put his arm around her.

"Not yet."

He laughed, kissing her, and gradually they moved until they were both lying down, facing each other. She broke away, laughing.

He lifted himself onto one elbow. "What's so funny?"

"You're a guy," she giggled. "And this is a bed."

"Not bad," he nodded. "You must be in Honors English."

"I've never done anything like this." She couldn't stop giggling. "I feel so weird. Now I can say I was in bed with a guy."

"*On* bed."

"Yeah, but still."

"You're so cute." He moved his head to kiss her and she laughed, turning away. "What are you doing?"

"I can't help it, it's too funny." With a concentrated effort, she swallowed the giggles. "Okay. I'm okay now."

He moved forward and the giggles came out again.

"Hey, what is this?" he asked, settling back on his elbow. "How can I kiss you if you keep laughing?"

She shrugged, laughing too hard to speak. He moved his head tentatively and she laughed harder.

"Fine." He rolled onto his back. "Reject me. See if I care."

"You wouldn't care?" she laughed.

"Nope. You kiss lousy."

She stopped laughing. "I do not."

"You do. It practically makes me throw up."

"It does not."

He laughed, seeing how offended she was.

"Fine," he said. "Prove me wrong."

She shook her head. "No, you're right. I won't kiss you again."

"Oh, God." He covered his eyes with one arm. "I'll kill myself."

"Would you really?"

"Yup." He hit himself in the chest. "Shove a knife right through my heart."

"Hey, that echoed!"

"What did?" He uncovered his eyes.

"When you did that." She bounced her fist gently off his chest. "Hear that? It echoes! That's really neat."

He nodded. "I'm kind of remarkable."

"Wow," she said, bouncing her fist again. "I wish I echoed."

"You don't?"

"I don't think so." She hit herself. "Nope. No echo."

"Can I check?"

"Nope." She grinned and kissed him. "There. Did that make you sick?"

"I'm not sure; try again."

She kissed him and they both laughed.

"You do it perfectly." He put his arms around her and they moved closer together.

"Hey," he said after a few minutes.

"What?" She didn't move her mouth from his.

"I'm, like, really hot. Will you get all hung up if I take off my shirt?"

"I don't think so," she said slowly.

"I'm just really hot." He stood up, unbuttoning from the top down, tossing the shirt on his desk chair.

As he turned around, Trish caught her breath without realizing she was doing it, staring at the lean muscles in his stomach, muscles rippling up to define his chest and shoulders, then down his arms, ending at familiar thin wrists, masculine wrists.

Glancing over, he laughed.

"God, you've got big eyes," he said.

Trish flushed, yanking her gaze away.

"No one ever—" She shook her head, embarrassed.

"You never saw a guy with his shirt off?"

"Never a guy with me." It was harder to jerk her eyes away this time. "Colin, could I—" She stopped.

"Could you what?"

"No, it's stupid." She hesitated. "Do you mind if I touch your stomach?"

He shook his head and she reached out her hand, sliding it across the muscles, feeling them tighten as he sucked in his breath.

"Uh, is there anything wrong with it?" he asked.

"No," she said quickly. "No, it's—it's beautiful."

"Beautiful?" He looked down.

"Really beautiful," she nodded.

"My stomach?"

She nodded again.

"Wow." He sucked it in a little more. "Wow, you really . . . ?" He sat down, putting his arm around her.

She touched it again, still hesitant.

"You're warm," she said.

"I think I have a fever."

She moved her hand up to his chest.

"It's so solid." She hit it to hear the echo. "It's really nice."

"Not too thin?" he asked nervously.

"It's perfect. Could I—" She withdrew again, embarrassed.

He moved her hair out of her face. "Could you what?"

"Could I listen to your heart for a second? I never listened to anyone's heart."

He nodded and she rested her head lightly against his chest, listening.

"It sounds so alive," she whispered.

He didn't say anything, trembling.

"Are you okay?" She sat up.

He nodded, visibly trembling.

"What's wrong?"

"No one ever—" He took a deep breath. "You sounded like it was—special."

"That you're alive?"

He nodded.

"Well, it is." She rested her fingertips just below the hollow where his collarbones met. "It's really special."

He closed his eyes, trembling.

"It's very special," she said softly.

"Cut it out. You'll make me cry."

"It would be okay." She moved her hand up to his cheek.

"Oh, Trish." He held it there, opening his eyes, which were very bright. "Would you sit on my lap? So I can hold you?"

She moved onto his lap and he put his arms around her, their heads resting against each other.

"Is it okay if we stay like this until you have to go?" He brushed his lips across her hair.

"I want to."

They were silent for a minute.

"You're breathing at the same time I am," she whispered.

"I know," he whispered back. "I can't help it." He held her closer. "Trish?"

"What?"

"I think you're special too."

CHAPTER NINETEEN

"You're sure it's okay we're going to this?" Colin hesitated as they arrived at Chuck Johnson's party on Friday night. Chuck was also in the play.

Trish laughed. "He invited you twice."

"Yeah, well—it looks crowded."

"Pretty many kids are coming," she agreed.

"Well, do I look like a jerk? I mean, what I'm wearing?"

"You look wonderful." She kissed him. "It's going to be fun, don't worry."

"Yeah, well—what if they don't want me?"

"Rachael's going to be there, and Janet, and Peter, and everyone. Come on," she said, pulling the door open. Loud music and voices blared out.

He hung back. "You don't ring the bell?"

"Everyone just walks in."

"Are his parents really here?"

"No," she admitted. "Mom and I have this game—she asks me if they're going to be there, I say I'm not sure, and we both know what we mean." She closed the door behind them and they both squinted in the darkened hall.

"Hey, hi." Chuck, going from the kitchen to the living room, paused when he saw them. " 'Bout time you guys got here. You can stick your coats up in that room," he said, pointing. "And there's all kinds of beer in the refrigerator."

"Thanks." Trish took off her jacket.

"Uh, Trish?" Colin whispered. "Would you get worked up if I, like, had some beer?"

"No." She paused. "How much beer?"

"I don't know." He put her jacket on the bed with all the

other jackets. "I don't mean I'm going to get blasted or anything; I just like beer. Does it bother you?"

"No."

"Want me to get you one too?"

"Maybe one," she said. "I don't usually have more than that."

"You probably wouldn't *need* more than that," he grinned, putting his hands on her waist.

There were several people in the kitchen, who all nodded and said hello. Colin took two beers out of the refrigerator, opened one, and gave it to Trish. In the room there was a girl on the phone, covering her other ear with her hand to shut out the noise of the party; a boy and a girl at the table, bent close in low, serious conversation; two boys sitting up on the counter.

"Heard rehearsals are going pretty well," one of the boys on the counter commented.

"They are," Trish agreed. "You want to work on the set? We still need people."

"Will I get my name in the program?"

She nodded.

"Maybe I'll do it then." He gulped the last of his beer. "I need more stuff on my applications. McNamara, you're closer, can you get me another?"

Colin shrugged and got out another beer.

"Where you applying?" Trish asked.

"I don't know," the boy said, popping the lid on the can. "Colby and UNH are the only two I know for sure. Probably BU too."

"What do you want to do?" Colin leaned against the refrigerator.

"I don't know. My father wants me to be a lawyer."

"Whose father doesn't?" the other boy on the counter asked.

Mike Pilsner and two of his friends came stumbling in to get more beer, already well on their way to getting drunk.

"What you doin' here?" Mike growled, shoving Colin out of his way.

Colin shoved right back.

"Hey, watch yourself, little boy." Mike got two more beers. "I might have to step on you."

"Yeah, I'd like to see you."

"Colin, why don't we go out here for a minute?" Trish grabbed his arm to pull him out of the kitchen.

"What are you doing?" Colin jerked free. "I was going to—"

"I know. Don't, okay? Please?"

"Yeah, well, if he—"

"Please, Colin?"

He scowled, but let his fists come apart.

"He just better stay out of my way," he muttered.

"Hey!" Peter came out from the living room, shouting over the music. "They want to hear you do, 'Ya Got Trouble.'"

"Who does?" Colin asked dubiously.

"Some kids in here. We were telling them about it."

"I don't want to."

"Yeah, you do." Trish pushed him forward.

"I really don't."

"Go entertain your fans."

"Aren't you coming with me?" he asked nervously.

"Oh, Trish, thank God you're here." Rachael hurried out. "I *have* to talk to you."

"Come on," Peter insisted, dragging Colin, who looked nervously back into the living room.

Rachael sat heavily on the stairs.

"What's wrong?" Trish sat next to her.

"He's here."

"Lance?" Trish asked. Rachael had a wild crush on Lance Williams, a boy in their history class.

Rachael nodded, her eyes closing.

"Who'd he come with?"

"Jim and those guys." She sat up. "Beth and Sarah have been all over him all night."

"Did you talk to him?"

"He said hi." Rachael fell back on her elbows. "I was too afraid to say anything else."

"You should go for it."

"But I look awful." She slumped down. "Could you ever like someone who had *glasses?*"

"You look good in glasses."

Rachael snorted.

"Well, you do."

"And this." Rachael pulled at her sweater. "I never would have worn it if I'd known he was coming. It's about as sultry as an onion sack." She stiffened. "Oh, my God."

Trish turned and saw a tall, well-muscled boy coming out into the hall, obviously looking for someone. Seeing Rachael, he headed toward them.

"I was looking for you." His voice was very deep. "Hi." He nodded at Trish, then looked back at Rachael. "You want a beer or something?"

"Sure," Rachael said weakly.

"Back in a minute." He walked toward the kitchen.

"Oh, my God," Rachael gasped. "What do I do?"

"Wait for him to come back."

"You're supposed to advise me."

"Well, go for it."

"Is that it?" Rachael shook her head. "This is terrible, I don't even know what to say to him."

"Cheer up," Trish said. "Maybe you won't have to say anything."

They both laughed, and Trish went into the living room, where she spotted Colin over by the fireplace, surrounded by girls. She paused, her arms going across her chest.

"Jealousy rears its ugly head," Janet said from behind her, sitting on a couch next to Peter.

Trish sat down next to them. "You'd better believe it."

"The new heartthrob of Curley High." Peter grinned.

"Hey, I'm not jealous." Trish tapped her foot. "It doesn't bother me at all."

The other two laughed.

"Hey, finally," Colin said a little while later, when he found her in the dining room talking to some people.

"Ran out of women, huh?" she asked.

"Yeah, I heard you were being jealous." He put his arms on her shoulders. "You know how stupid that is?"

"No." She shook her head, arms going around his waist. "I'm not a brain."

"I guess not." He kissed her. "I thought the parties I *used* to go to were wild. Will you wait if I go get a beer?"

"Maybe."

"I'll be right back." He kissed her again.

"Okay."

"Hey, Trish?" a girl asked, passing her a minute later. "You wouldn't happen to have any bobby pins, would you?"

"Yeah, I think I've got some in my coat," Trish said. "I'll go look."

"Oh, I meant with you. Don't go to any—"

"It isn't," Trish assured her. "Just tell Colin where I went if he gets here before I get back."

The girl nodded, and Trish made her way through the crowd to the room where the coats were. She went through the pile, trying to find her ski jacket. Just as she located it, the light suddenly went off and she heard the door close.

"Hey, what's going on?" She spun around.

There was a low chuckle and she tried not to panic, swallowing the automatic bubble of fear.

"Come on, who is it?" she asked, making her voice sound normal.

"Thought you were used to dark bedrooms," the voice laughed.

Trish gulped, recognizing it despite the drunken slur.

"Come on, Mike, it's not funny," she said. "Turn it back on; I have to get something."

He laughed again, flipping the light on.

"Whatsa matter?" he asked, a beer in one hand, another in his shirt pocket. "Did I scare you?"

"No," Trish lied, even more scared as she saw how drunk he was, saw how really big he was.

"I scared hell out of you." He finished the beer in his hand and opened the other.

"A little," she admitted. "I'd better get back out there, people'll wonder where I am."

"No one'll notice."

"Well, I told Beth—"

"Cut it, okay?" He drained half the beer. "I wanna talk to you."

"W-we, we can't talk out there?"

"I don't wanna talk out there." He turned the lock on the door.

Trish flinched as it clicked.

"Scared?" he asked.

"No." She backed up, terrified, as he came closer. This was Mike Pilsner, she'd known him since junior high. He wasn't going to do anything, he couldn't— "I-I really have to go back out there."

"Let's see you try it." His muscles bulged and he blocked her way to the door, dropping his now empty beer can.

She stared at him, paralyzed, seeing mostly the huge, threatening hands.

"Come on, Trish." He took another step, cornering her. "Let's see your stuff."

"If you come any closer," her voice shook, "I'll scream."

"No one'll hear you."

"They'll hear me." She felt the wall on both sides and gulped, struggling not to panic, telling herself that she knew him, that he couldn't possibly—she gulped again, hearing her heart slamming against her ears.

One side of his mouth lifted in a sneer.

"Scared?" he asked.

She shook her head, realizing suddenly that she wasn't, that all she was was angry.

"Yeah, you are. I can tell you are." He tangled one hand in her hair. "Come on, I wanna—"

"Get off me!" She jerked away from him. "You can't do this to me!"

"Wanna bet?" He came closer. "Come on," he said, putting his hands on her shoulders. "All I wanna do is kiss you."

"Well, you can't!" Trish shook his hands off and ducked past him to the door.

"Get back here!" He grabbed for her and missed.

"Try and make me," Trish said, unlocking the door and running out to the hall.

"Hey, there you are," Colin said, on his way out of the living room. "I've been looking all over for you."

"You found me," Trish said, feeling herself trembling now that she was out of the room and safe.

"Are you okay?" He frowned at her. "You look funny."

"I'm fine." She took his arm. "Come on, let's go back in the other room."

"You're sure you're okay?"

"I'm fine, don't worry. Come on, let's just—"

Mike came out of the bedroom, his face stiff, shoving past them on his way to the kitchen and another beer. Colin stared at Mike disappearing into the crowd spilling out of the living room, then at Trish.

"What happened?" he demanded.

"Nothing," Trish said quickly.

"He was in there with you. What happened?"

"Nothing."

"Did he try anything? Did he—"

"No. We just both happened to be—"

Colin turned around, striding toward the living room.

"Colin, don't!" Trish went after him. "I'm fine. Nothing happened."

He didn't answer, hurrying through the crowd, and Trish tried to keep up with him.

"Hey, Trish," Becky Geer said, putting her hand out to stop her. "I wanted to ask you—"

"I can't really talk right now," Trish interrupted. "I kind of have to—"

"It'll only take a second," Becky said. "I just wanted to know if—"

"I'm sorry, I can't." Trish scanned the crowd, not seeing Colin anywhere. She pushed her way through to the kitchen, didn't see Colin or Mike, and hurried back to the living room, still not seeing them. Scared, she struggled through the crush of people to the dining room.

"What's wrong?" Peter asked.

"I can't find Colin. Have you seen Colin?" Trish squinted around the dimly lit room, trying not to sound as nervous as she felt.

"I don't know," Peter said, also looking. "He has to be around here somewhere. Is anything wrong?"

"I think he went after Mike."

"What?" Peter stared at her. "Why would he do that?"

"He thinks Mike was bothering me."

"Was he?"

"Yeah. I guess he's pretty drunk."

Peter snapped into action. "You go that way," he said, pointing toward the kitchen, "and I'll go this way."

"I just looked in there," Trish said.

"Check again," Peter said, heading for the living room.

In the meantime, Colin had stormed out to the front hall, grabbing the first person he ran into.

"Hey! You seen Pilsner?" he asked, furious.

"Y-yeah," the boy nodded, a little unnerved. "He just went outside with Burt and Sam."

"Thanks." Colin strode to the front door, where he saw Mike and his two friends slouched on the front steps with beers in each hand. He yanked off his sweater and stepped outside, closing the door hard behind him. All three boys looked up.

"Hey, the tramp's boyfriend," Burt, another football player, sneered.

Colin jumped on him, knocking him off the front steps, and they were in the front walk struggling.

"Let's get him," Mike growled.

Colin scrambled free, backing up, crouched low, both fists ready.

"I'll take you one at a time," he panted. "Or all at once. Whatever you want."

"You got all of us, then." Mike circled him with the two other boys, waiting for someone to make the first move. "You're gonna get smashed, McNamara."

"You get something clear." Colin kept moving, his weight balanced, trying to watch all three at once. "Don't go near her again. I don't want you talking to her, or looking at her, or anything."

"Be kinda hard with a tramp like that," Mike jeered.

Colin jumped on him, fists swinging. As Mike went down, the other two boys rushed him, but Colin ignored them, concentrating on Mike, infuriated, his breath coming in jerking gasps. One, or both, of the others, got his arms behind his back and he struggled to get free, trying to avoid the fists Mike kept slamming at him. He almost wrenched away, but Mike hit him deep in the stomach and he groaned, doubling over, his breath gone. All three were at him, but he managed to stay on his feet, swinging, not sure if he was connecting.

"Hey!" Peter shouted from the door, seeing the one-sided battle. "Someone go get Chuck!" He shouted into the house. "And anyone else you can find!" He ran down the steps, jumping on Burt and dragging him away from the struggle.

The odds that much lessened, Colin gave Sam a hard elbow to the jaw, momentarily stunning him, and kept after Mike, taking three to the face, but getting in two of his own.

Most of the party came running outside to see the fight, and it took five of the boys to break it up. Colin ripped away from the two holding him, swaying on his feet, but fists still up.

"I'll take on all of you if I have to!" His voice was thick. "I'll—"

"Colin." Peter hadn't moved back with the others.

"I'll start with you, Peter!"

"Let's go inside," Peter suggested. "You're in pretty bad shape."

"I'm not done with him." Colin tried to focus on the group and find Mike. "Come on, Pilsner! Let's finish it!"

"Let go of me." Mike fought at the boys keeping him back. "Lemme smash the twerp!"

"Let's see you try!" Colin yelled. "Come on!" He motioned him over with his fists.

"Colin," Peter tried again.

"I gotta! He can't do that to her! Come on, Pilsner!"

"I'll kill 'im!" Mike growled, breaking free.

Colin had his fists up, ready to face the charge, when Mike stopped short.

"Come on!" Colin shouted dizzily.

"You call that a fair fight?" Mike asked, his expression sour.

"Huh?" Colin turned, looking twice as startled as Mike when he saw Peter and Chuck, as well as several other boys from their English class, right behind him.

"It's as fair as three against one," Peter said. "Come on, Pilsner, let's see you kill him."

"Wh-what are you doing?" Colin was still stunned.

"Backing you up," Chuck said, scowling at Mike.

"But—I mean—he's your friend."

"Since when?" a boy asked.

"Yeah, you're really a jerk, Pilsner," another boy agreed. "This kid's got more guts than all three of you guys."

"Why don't you just get out of here?" a third suggested.

Looking equally startled, neither Mike nor Colin moved.

"Oh, no," Chuck groaned, seeing a car with flashing red lights pull up. "My parents are going to kill me."

The whole group got very quiet as the two policemen got out and swaggered up the walk, nightsticks out.

"What's going on here?" one demanded.

No one made a sound except for Colin, who grinned.

"Hey, Bucky," he said. "How ya doin'?"

"Colin, what are you doing here?" The cop lowered his stick.

Colin shrugged. "We heard fire trucks, so we came outside. Were we making too much noise?"

"We got three calls." The cop nodded. "Said there was a fight going on."

"Not around here," Colin said.

"Then what happened to you?"

"Fell down the steps when we were running out," Colin said, pointing.

"How'd you manage that?"

Colin put on his best grin. "I'm Irish. I drink too much."

"That's a McNamara for you." The cop had to smile.

"It's getting pretty late," the other cop said. "How about you all break this up?"

"Hey, Fred, this is Jerry McNamara's son," the first cop said. "Colin, this is Fred."

"Hi." Colin shook his hand. "Don't worry about a thing. There won't be any noise from here. You guys better get going and find some *real* trouble."

"Okay," Bucky said. "I'm making *you* responsible."

"Yes, sir!" Colin saluted. "Thank you, sir!"

"Jerry's gonna love this." Bucky went back to the car, shaking his head.

No one said anything as the two police officers got back into their car and drove away. Chuck broke the silence.

"Maybe you ought to get going, Pilsner," he said.

"Yeah, right," Mike said shortly. "Funny how you find out who your friends are."

"Real funny," Chuck agreed.

As Mike and his two friends headed grumblingly for their car, people started inside.

"You okay, McNamara?" a boy asked.

"Uh, yeah." Colin nodded. "Thanks."

"You *are* okay," another boy said, passing him.

"Uh, thanks." Colin glanced at Peter, who grinned at him.

"Us 'bang-beat, bell-ringin', big-haul, great-go, neck-or-nothin', rip-roarin', ever'-time-a-bull's-eye salesmen' gotta stick together, y'know?" Peter said.

"No, I didn't," Colin said.

"You do now."

"Hey." Trish finally got through to him. "Are you all right? Oh, Colin." She touched his face.

"Forget me." He winced slightly away from her hand. "Are you okay?"

"I'm fine," she said, putting her arm around his waist to support him. "Are you?"

"Yeah." He leaned on her in spite of himself, Peter moving in to support his other side. Colin smiled shyly at him. "Yeah, I think I am."

CHAPTER TWENTY

After going inside so Colin could wash his face and Trish could get their coats, they left the party, refusing Peter's offer of a ride. From Chuck's apartment on Beacon Street, they walked over to Commonwealth, arms around each other's waists.

"Are you sure you're okay?" Trish asked.

"I'm fine." He kissed the side of her head. "How about you?"

Trish smiled. "I feel great," she said.

"Yeah? Me too."

They stopped in front of her brownstone, facing each other, arms on each other's shoulders now.

"Can you make it home okay?" Trish asked.

"Sure. I've been in fights before."

"Will you do me a favor and take a cab home?"

"I'm fine; I can walk."

"Here," she said, reaching into her pocket and taking out some money. "It's on me."

"Don't be dumb." He pushed her hand away.

"Please? It would make me happy."

He laughed. "Would it?"

"It really would." She nodded.

"Okay." He kissed her. "I'll make you happy."

They embraced.

"You always make me happy," Trish said against his mouth.

"Yeah? So do you."

They kissed again.

"Does it hurt you to do this?" Trish asked.

"Hell, no."

They broke apart finally, both out of breath.

"I'd better get home and put on some ice," he said, leaning his head against hers.

"Do you want to come in and get some here?"

"No, it's pretty late." He gave her a lingering kiss. "See you tomorrow?"

"Yeah." She saw a taxi coming up Commonwealth and lifted her arm to stop it.

As the taxi pulled over to the curb, they kissed one more time.

"You know what? I was really proud of you tonight," she whispered.

"I was kind of a jerk to start all that trouble."

"Yeah," she agreed. "I still thought you were wonderful."

"You know what?" he said. "You're pretty great yourself."

They kissed one final time, then Colin climbed into the backseat of the cab.

"Call me in the morning," she said before he closed the door.

"I will."

Trish watched the cab pull away before turning to go up her front steps, fumbling for her doorkey.

Inside her house, she sank exhausted onto the stairs, leaning forward, arms resting on her knees.

"Oh, good, I'm glad you're home." Her mother came out into the hall, holding a theater history textbook in one hand. "Did you have a good time?"

Trish groaned and buried her head in her arms.

"Are you okay? What happened?"

"Everything." Trish didn't pick her head up.

Mrs. Masters smiled and sat down next to her, not too worried.

"Now, let me guess." She put her arm around her daughter. "Everyone got really drunk, a bunch of fights started, and the police had to come and break the thing up."

"My God." Trish sat up, staring at her. "That's incredible."

"You mean, that happened?" It was her mother's turn to stare.

"Uh, no, no, of course not." Trish realized that she'd made a mistake. "I'm just tired. Think I'll go to bed."

"You're not going anywhere," her mother said, pulling her down, "until you tell me what happened."

"Nothing happened."

"What, do you think I'll get mad?" Mrs. Masters asked. "Was there drinking?"

Trish just rolled her eyes.

"Okay, dumb question," her mother said. "Were *you* drinking?"

Trish rolled her eyes again.

"Guess I'm two for two." Mrs. Masters moved her jaw. "Was Colin drinking?"

"No." Trish stood up. "I really have to go to bed, Mom. I'm so tired I'm going to die."

"If you don't sit down and tell me what happened, I'll save you the trouble."

"Okay, okay." Trish stayed standing. "It really wasn't that bad. Things were just getting kind of wild, some guy made a crack at me, and Colin got in a fight with him. A neighbor called the police because it was kind of noisy, but it was okay, because they work with Colin's father, so he knew them, and they left."

"Did Colin get hurt in the fight?"

"A black eye and stuff." She shrugged. "He's fine. I'm fine. Everything's fine." She started up the stairs. "Think I'll go to bed."

"You, you do that," her mother said, trying to assimilate the story.

"Are you mad?"

"I just have this feeling you left things out."

"Probably," Trish agreed.

"I figured." Her mother nodded. "Are you going to tell me?"

"Probably not."

"I figured." Standing up, Mrs. Masters let her breath out in a sigh. "I'm not altogether sure why I let you go to these things." She picked up her book. "Just tell me one thing. Were his parents really there?"

"I didn't really see them," Trish admitted. "They might have been upstairs."

"Probably padlocked in the attic," Mrs. Masters said wryly.

"Oh, no, now I remember." Trish kept her back to her mother, hiding her grin. "They were busted because of the drugs."

"What drugs, Patricia?"

"Boy, am I tired." Trish got to the top of the stairs, yawning widely. "See you in the morning." She escaped down the hall to her room.

In school on Monday, everyone was very cordial to Colin, though keeping a quiet, respectful distance.

"This is pretty fun." He grinned as he moved down the hall with Trish and people got out of their way. "They think I'm kind of an animal, huh?"

"How little they know."

"The sadder but wiser girl for me." Then, he winced. "Miss Slater's going to kill me. I'm probably not supposed to go out and get beat up when I'm working on a show."

"Probably not." She put her arm around his waist. "But you'll heal by the time the show goes up."

"I better."

"You're just lucky you didn't break anything."

"Yeah, really." He paused as they got to his Spanish room. "Guess I'll see you in chemistry." He stared down at his books. "What am I doing in these classes?"

"You're a brain."

"I'm not so sure."

"Face it, kid." She released him. "You've come out of the closet."

"Huh?" He jumped, glancing around to make sure no one else had heard. "What do you mean?"

"Closet intellectual, remember?"

"Oh, yeah. Well, at least they didn't stick me in trig."

"Next year."

"Terrific." He went into his classroom. "Later."

"Right." Trish continued down the hall.

"Hey, Trish!"

Seeing Mike Pilsner coming toward her, his mouth and right eye swollen, she stiffened.

"Look, I'm sorry," he said, his voice flippantly defensive.

"Sorry?"

"Yeah. I was drunk, y'know?"

"Drunk," she said.

"Yeah. What are you, deaf?"

She shook her head, the anger that had started on Friday night flowing back, twice as strong.

"I wouldn't've hurt you or anything," he said.

"You didn't get a chance."

"For chrissakes, I was drunk!"

"Terrific," she said. "You were drunk." She turned and started walking down the hall.

"I said I was sorry!" he shouted after her.

"So what if you're sorry?" She saw Rachael hurrying over from her locker. "Don't worry, we're not late."

Rachael glanced down toward Mike. "Is everything okay?" she asked.

"Sure," Trish said. "Why wouldn't it be?"

"I don't know," Rachael said. "No reason."

"No reason," Trish agreed cheerfully. She looked around the emptying hall as the bell rang. "We'd better get moving to class."

Rachael nodded and followed her.

* * *

At rehearsal that afternoon, Miss Slater saw Colin coming in. She gasped.

"What happened?" she asked.

"Got in a fight."

"Are you all right? Can you sing?"

"I can even dance." He grinned. "I protected my throat too."

"How long will it take for those bruises to go away?"

"Dunno. Couple of weeks, I guess."

She sat down, shaking her head. "Will you do me a favor?"

"What?"

"Promise you'll be careful until the show? That you won't let anything happen? There isn't anyone who could take your part."

"Trish could do it. She's got it memorized."

"Yeah, I'd be great." Trish had heard him from the stage, where she was setting up the rehearsal furniture. "They call me the sadder but wiser girl."

"Who does that?" Colin doubled up his fists. "I'll smack him!"

"Don't you dare!" Miss Slater grabbed his arm. "Don't you dare get in a fight! Don't walk into trees, don't fall down stairs—don't do anything!"

"I won't." He started to jump onto the stage, but purposely didn't go high enough and fell onto the floor.

"My God, are you all right?" Miss Slater leaped up.

"Yeah." He winked at her. "I'm just a show-off."

Rehearsals intensified as the days passed, and suddenly it was the first of two dress rehearsals.

"There, that's good." Trish fixed the tie on his first-act costume.

"I look all right?" He studied the mirror.

"You look beautiful."

"Thanks a lot." He grimaced.

"You didn't blot your lipstick."

"Cut it out." He pushed her away, blushing.

"You do look good in eye makeup, though."

"I said, cut it out." He put his arms on her shoulders. "What are you doing Thursday night?"

"Pacing around and worrying about Friday."

"How about going out with me? I got tickets to a play, and I thought we could get all dressed up, go out to dinner—"

"Friday's opening night, you have to go to bed early."

"We won't stay out late. I just feel like celebrating, that's all. Your mother already said it was okay."

"When'd you talk to her?"

"Sunday. Come on, they're mezzanine and everything."

"That's so expensive," she breathed. "You shouldn't have . . ."

"No problem," he said, gesturing expansively with one arm. "I'm independently wealthy."

"I'm serious." She straightened his collar. "I hate it when you try to pay for everything. I worked all summer, I have money."

"You didn't make eight dollars an hour."

She stopped straightening. "You made eight dollars an hour?"

"My father got me a job working construction." He put on his father's voice and expression. "I'm thinking I want you to beef out a little, lad. You're too thin." He flexed his arms, then grinned. "And look at me. Now I wear lipstick."

"I think you look cute." She smiled. "It brings out your—"

"Places." Martha, the stage manager, stuck her head in. "They need you backstage, Trish. The Act Two drop's all screwed up."

"I'm on my way." She gave Colin a careful hug, not wanting to mess up his costume. "Break a leg."

He grinned on his way out to the stage, kissing her collar to leave a lipstick mark.

CHAPTER TWENTY-ONE

When Trish hurried downstairs on Thursday night, Colin had already been there for over twenty minutes. He stood up as she came into the living room. She stared at him. He was tall and dark in a gray suit with a well-coordinated tie and crisp Oxford shirt, and he held a bouquet of daisies.

"You look wonderful," he said softly.

"So do you."

"Oh, here." He handed her the flowers.

"Thank you, they're beautiful."

"Next to you, they look like crab grass." He ran his eyes down, admiring the black-velvet blazer, gray pleated skirt with thin lines of black and blue, the shapely black boots. "We even match." He touched her arm. "That's a beautiful blazer."

"It's Mom's." Trish grinned at her mother. "If anything happens to it, I'm not supposed to come home."

"I'll protect you." Colin glanced at his watch. "We'd better get going so we'll make our reservations."

"Have a good time," Mrs. Masters said, following them to the door.

When they were standing on the sidewalk, looking at each other, they both felt awkward, unfamiliar.

"So," Trish said.

"Right," Colin agreed.

They exchanged shy glances, then he straightened his shoulders, extending his arm into the street.

"Taxi!" he shouted.

"We could walk," Trish said without conviction.

"No way. I owe you one." He pulled open the back door of the cab that slowed for them, letting her get in first, then climbing in and giving the driver the address. He sat back and took her hand. "You really look beautiful."

"I love your suit."

"My parents got it for me when they figured I'd stopped growing." He grinned. "If I start again, I think I'll kill myself."

"Don't do that."

"Well, if it'd upset you, I won't." He lifted her hand to his lips. "I have to watch myself tonight. Miss Slater said I'd better make sure nothing happened to me. So, like, if you get mugged, I have to keep walking."

"And leave me there?"

"Yeah, sorry."

"Thanks a lot."

"You know I'm kidding. Just do me a favor and stay away from muggers tonight."

"I'll try."

Inside the restaurant, they were seated at a small table by the window, high above the city; outside, the lights were bright in the winter darkness.

"It's so beautiful," Trish whispered.

"Really beautiful," he agreed.

"You're not even looking out the window."

"It's nice out there too."

"You know," Trish covered his hand with hers. "I can't think of anywhere else in the world I'd rather be."

"Neither can I." He lifted her hand to kiss it. "One thing," he said. "We're not mentioning money at all, okay?"

"But—"

"I'm only going to say it once." He opened his menu. "We are suave and sophisticated."

"We are?"

"Tonight."

"Would either of you care for a cocktail?" their waiter asked, pen poised.

"Yes," Colin said. "That would be nice. Trish?"

"Uh, well, I—I—" She found her mind a blank.

"How about a carafe of white wine?" Colin said to the waiter.

"The house wine, sir?"

"Yes." Colin nodded. "That'll be fine, thank you."

"You sound like someone out of *The Great Gatsby*," she whispered as the waiter left.

"Yeah?" He straightened his tie. "Then it's working."

"Working?"

"I was trying for Gatsby." He paused. "You really are beautiful."

"So are you," she said.

He smiled, bringing her hand to his mouth and kissing it.

"I can't wait until tomorrow," she said.

He sighed. "I can."

"You're going to be wonderful."

"I'm . . ." He stared out the window, embarrassed, "kind of scared to death."

"I know. You're going to be great, though."

"I've, like, been waiting for this my whole life," he said.

"I know."

"I-I'm really scared."

"I know," she said. "But—"

"Are you ready to order?" their waiter asked, arriving with the carafe.

Colin shook his head, snapping out of it. "Uh, no, no, I don't think we are," he said, suave and sophisticated again. "Could you give us a few minutes?"

"Yes, sir." The waiter set down the glasses, poured some wine in each, and left.

"Gatsby returns." Trish grinned.

Colin grinned back, then concentrated on his menu.

After spending as much time as they could over dinner, then seeing a play that was previewing on its way to Broadway, they were out on the street, under a clear, star-filled sky.

"That was wonderful," Trish said.

"Yeah." Colin nodded. "That guy was really good."

She slid her arm through his. "You're going to be even better."

"Don't even talk about it," he said. "Just keep your eyes out for muggers."

"Oh, right." She leaned against him and he put his arm around her. "Isn't it beautiful out?"

"I'm surrounded." He looked up at the sky. "How about we walk partway? It's still early."

She smiled. "I know, I was giving you a hint."

They walked slowly, enjoying the night, enjoying each other, slowing more as they turned onto Arlington Street, headed for Commonwealth Avenue.

" 'There were bells on the hill, but I never heard them ringing,' " he sang. " 'No, I never heard them at all, till there was you.' "

"Practicing for tomorrow?" Trish laughed.

"I'm being romantic."

"Oh, is that it."

" 'There were birds in the sky, but I never saw them winging, no, I never saw them at all, till there was—' "

Trish laughed and started across the street. Colin, who was in the middle of a romantic bow, glanced up to see where she'd gone and froze, seeing the car hurtling toward her.

"Trish!" he shouted.

She turned, startled, but was still in the street, still in the path of the car.

He knew he wasn't going to be able to move, knew he couldn't get out there to save her, knew he couldn't—and then, was in the street, shoving her out of the way, finding himself staring into headlights.

There was a terrifying screech of brakes and he felt rushing wind as the car skidded around him, somehow missed him. He stumbled up against a mailbox on the sidewalk, gasping, still seeing headlights, perspiration coursing down his face. He managed to lift his head and saw that she was also out of breath, leaning against a telephone pole, equally shaken up.

"Are you all right?" he demanded.

"Thank you for pushing me," she said weakly.

"Are you okay?"

"I'm fine."

He leaned on the mailbox, resting his head on his arms, reaction trembling hitting hard.

"Colin?" she asked uneasily.

"Do you know how stupid that was?" he snapped.

"I didn't mean to."

"Well, it was really stupid." He wiped a shaking arm across his face. "Really, really stupid."

"I'm sorry."

"You almost got killed and you're *sorry?*" His sleeve went back across his face again. "Can we go sit down somewhere for a minute?"

"Over there?" She gestured toward the Public Gardens.

He nodded, then started tensing up again, realizing that they would have to cross the street.

"You okay?" she asked, putting her hand on his back.

"Of course I am! Did I say I wasn't?" He stared at the Walk/Don't Walk indicator. "I'm fine."

When the red Don't Walk changed to a white Walk, she automatically took his hand.

"What, am I four years old?" he asked, jerking free. He took an almost unnoticeable deep breath. "Come on."

"Colin?"

He turned impatiently. "What?"

"Can I tell you something?"

"What?"

"I love you."

"What—is that supposed to give me courage?"

"I don't know."

"Yeah, well, I'm not scared. I can do it." He took her hand back. "Come on."

They crossed the street, getting to the other side just as the

Don't Walk started flashing. Without a pause, they headed into the park, where they sat on a very dark, very quiet bench, still tightly holding hands.

"You shouldn't have done it," she said after a minute.

"Done what?" He was still trembling a little.

"Jumped out in the street like that. Miss Slater would throw a fit."

"Are you nuts?" He stared at her. "You think I care about the stupid show? What's the stupid show matter? You're the one who—" He stopped, his expression scared, as if he'd said too much.

She looked at him, then moved over, and he put his arm around her and pulled her very close.

"Colin?"

He tightened his arm. "What?"

"I meant what I said."

"What?"

"That I—" She swallowed, the words seeming more important now that it was so quiet. "That I love you."

"Y-you do?" He looked down at her, his face softening.

"I really do." She nodded, knowing that she really did.

"Yeah?" He lifted a frightened hand to touch her face, moving her hair back, not saying anything. "Trish?" he asked finally.

"What?"

He took a deep breath, then stared at her for a minute.

"What?" She smiled, loving him.

"I—" He stopped, licking his lips. "I—Oh, God." He closed his eyes, hugging her to him. "Trish?"

"What?"

"I love you too," he whispered.

ELLEN EMERSON WHITE grew up in Naragansett, Rhode Island. She is currently a senior at Tufts University where she is pursuing a double major in English and education.

Flare Romance Novels

LOVECRAZY Judy Felffer 84160-6/$2.25
When two Manhattan teenage temptresses decide that their divorced mothers are weak in matters of the heart—they decide to learn from the best role models for romance—each other's fathers!

ROMANCE IS A WONDERFUL THING 83907-5/$2.25
Ellen Emerson White
Trish Masters, honor student, tennis player and all-around preppy is surprised when she falls in love with handsome Colin McNamara—the class clown.

I LOVE YOU, STUPID! Harry Mazer 61432-4/$2.50
Marcus Rosenbloom, an irresistible high school senior whose main problem is being a virgin, learns that neither sex, nor friendship—nor love—is ever very simple.

RECKLESS Jeanette Mines Ryan 83717-X/$2.25
Fourteen-year-old Jeannie Tanger discovers the pain and bittersweetness of first love when her romance with school troublemaker Sam Bensen alienates her from her friends and family.

SOONER OR LATER 61275-5/$2.25
Bruce and Carole Hart
When 13-year-old Jessie falls for Michael Skye, the handsome, 17-year-old leader of The Skye Band, she's sure he'll never be interested in her if he knows her true age.

WAITING GAMES 79012-2/$2.50
Bruce and Carole Hart
Although Jessie loves Michael more than ever, he wants more from her. Jessie must make a decision. How much is she willing to share with Michael—the man she's sure she'll love forever?

 FLARE Paperbacks

Available wherever paperbacks are sold or directly from the publisher. Include 50¢ per copy for postage and handling; allow 6-8 weeks for delivery. Avon Books, Mail Order Dept., 224 W. 57th St., N.Y., N.Y. 10019

NOVELS FROM AVON/FLARE

I LOVE YOU, STUPID!
Harry Mazer   61432-4/$2.50
Marcus Rosenbloom is a high school senior whose main problem in life is being a virgin. His dynamic relationship with the engaging Wendy Barrett, and his continuing efforts to "become a man," show him that neither sex, nor friendship—nor love—is ever very simple.

CLASS PICTURES
Marilyn Sachs   61408-1/$1.95
When shy, plump Lolly Scheiner arrives in kindergarten, she is the "new girl everyone hates," and only popular Pat Maddox jumps to her defense. From then on they're best friends through thick and thin, supporting each other during crises until everything changes in eighth grade, when Lolly suddenly turns into a thin, pretty blonde and Pat, an introspective science whiz, finds herself playing second fiddle for the first time.

JACOB HAVE I LOVED
Katherine Paterson   56499-8/$1.95
Do you ever feel that no one understands you? Louise's pretty and talented twin sister, Caroline, has always been the favored one, while Louise is ignored and misunderstood. Now Louise feels that Caroline has stolen from her all that she has ever wanted...until she learns how to fight for the love, and the life she wants for herself. "Bloodstirring." *Booklist* A Newbery Award-winner.

Available wherever paperbacks are sold or directly from the publisher. Include 50¢ per copy for postage and handling: allow 6-8 weeks for delivery. Avon Books, Mail Order Dept., 224 W. 57th St., N.Y., N.Y. 10019

NOVELS FROM AVON/FLARE

THE GROUNDING OF GROUP 6
by Julian Thompson

Coming in May 1983!
83386-7/$2.50

What do parents do when they realize that their sixteen-year old son or daughter is a loser and an embarassment to the family? If they are wealthy and have contacts, they can enroll their kids in Group 6 of the exclusive Coldbrook Country School, and the eccentric, diabolical Dr. Simms will make sure that they become permanently "grounded"—that is, murdered. When the five victims discover they are destined to "disappear"— and that their parents are behind the evil plot—they enlist the help of Nat, their group leader, to escape.

AFTER THE FIRST DEATH
by Robert Cormier   62885-6/$2.50

This shattering thriller is about a group of terrorists who hijack a school bus in New England and hold a group of children hostage—forcing each one to make decisions that will affect not only their own lives, but also the nation. "Marvelously told...The pressure mounts steadily." *The New York Times* "Haunting...Chilling ...Tremendous." *Boston Globe*

TAKING TERRI MUELLER
by award-winning Norma Fox Mazer   79004-1/$2.25

Was it possible to be kidnapped by your own father? For as long as Terri could remember, she and her father had been a family—alone together. Her mother had died nine years ago in a car crash—so she'd been told. But now Terri has reason to suspect differently, and as she struggles to find the truth on her own, she is torn between the two people she loves most.

Available wherever paperbacks are sold or directly from the publisher. Include 50¢ per copy for postage and handling: allow 6-8 weeks for delivery. Avon Books, Mail Order Dept., 224 W. 57th St., N.Y., N.Y. 10019